THE LAST SHEPHERD

A RURAL NOVEL

Set in Dumfries & Galloway

By

Miller Caldwell

Society of Authors

Adapted from a story by Jim Ramsay and now a film
script found at:
www.millercaldwell.org/filmscripts
Open for Option.

© Netherholm Publications

British Library Cataloguing Publication Data.
A catalogue record for this book is available from the British Library

ISBN 978-07552-0641-4

Authors OnLine Ltd
19 The Cinques
Gamlingay, Sandy
Bedfordshire SG19 3NU
England

This book is also available in e-book format, details of which are available at www.authorsonline.co.uk

Introduction.

A film script sometimes materialises out of a cartoon, news item, book or novel. Rarely, if ever, does a film script give birth to a novel. This novel is a rare exception. Books and film scripts have very different formats. The film script is precise, with fewer words at the expense of scene setting, of nuance, and of camera instruction. It is a very visual art form and it is highly formatted by genre. Language is kept to a minimum.

The novel on the other hand has scope to expand. It is designed to enthral the reader's mind. A novel enables a reader to experience and enjoy their personal interpretation of a book.

In the summer of 2008, from the Castle Douglas Lodge of Kelton farm, Jim Ramsay, brought this story to the attention of the Gracefield Arts studio. They arranged that I should make a film script of the work and that has now been completed. To compliment the film script, I have adapted the story into this novella. In doing so I have made no changes to Jim's storyline but have altered some names, expanded the narrative and exercised the author's prerogative in this contemporary Scots novel.

Miller H. Caldwell graduated from London University's School of Oriental and African Studies after he had spent six years in Ghana as Secretary to the Tema Council of Churches. He is the former Regional Reporter to the Dumfries and Galloway Children's Hearings. In London in 2002 he was awarded the inter-agency Community Care Award. He is a direct descendant of the poet Robert Burns and a Founding Fellow of the Institute of Contemporary Scotland. Since 2003 he has been a full time writer.

In Islamabad in 2006 he received the International Award for services to the Earthquake victims by Muslim Hands International. He had been the Camp Manager at Mundihar, in the North West Frontier Province of Pakistan.

He is the author of ten books and several film scripts. Details of his published works, travel photos, short stories and poetry appear on his website at www.millercaldwell.org and at the back of this book. He lives in Dumfries in south west Scotland with his wife.

Jim Ramsay was born in the farmhouse he lives in. He has farmed at Lodge of Kelton for 30 years. He left school at 15 years old. He was in the Dumfries & Galloway Mountain Rescue team for 10 years but retired after being attacked by a bull. He is married to Ginger and they have two sons.

Ginger is a farmer's daughter from Wales. She is a keen gardener and cook, making all her own jams and chutneys. Ginger works on the farm as well and being in charge of hand rearing the calves.

Robert is 10 and Hamish is 8 as this story goes for publication. They both play for Galloway Cricket Club. Both boys are interested in living at the farm.

Now let's meet the Last Shepherd and his antagonist, the Banker.

The Last Shepherd and the Banker.

Fresh grass everywhere and underneath the hoof
Salt licking blocks and troughs of natural water
Streams of trout await to be guddled out by hand
Crossed wires seeking a flow, are getting hotter

The banker relaxes in a strange rural environment
Where time records pennies, not crisp teners
Where the community works for each other
Alien city concepts clash then learn county manners.

Fields of yellow barley grow to please him
At sun down in Surrey with his glass in hand
Cowhide leather on his feet and on the sofa
Lessons learned painfully from a rural land.

© miller caldwell

Acknowledgements

I thank Jim Ramsay for bringing this story to the attention of Mark Geddes and Alice Stilgoe of the Dumfries & Galloway Film and Arts Council. That led to the film script. Now as a novella, I am grateful to Alan Nicolson and Lesley Fudge for providing helpful reviews of the script. Finally my personal thanks to Police Constable Ewan Grierson of the Dumfries & Galloway Pipe Band for his commitment to quality piping at various events in our community and as it happens, as a guest in this novel.

Dedicated

To Jim, Ginger, Robert and Hamish

At The Lodge of Kelton.

A Select Scots Glossary of words found in the text.

Awa	*away*
Ben	*through*
Braw	*handsome*
Byke	*swarm*
Canty	*cheerful*
Claes	*clothes*
Croudie-time	*breakfast*
Crouse	*merry*
Dondie	*unlucky*
Dool	*sorrow*
Drouth	*thirst*
Fash	*bother*
Fissle	*rustle*
Gar	*make*
Gash	*smart*
Gawsie	*ample*
Glakit	*foolish*
Gowans	*daisies*
Heapet	*well-filled*
Hurdies	*buttocks*
Ilka	*each and every*
Ken	*know*
Laverock	*skylark*
Leeze	*delight*
Lugs	*ears*
Meikle	*large, great*
Ram-stam	*headstrong*
Roose	*agitate*
Sconner	*sicken*
Sonsie	*comely*
Thae	*those*
Wheesht	*quiet*

CONTENTS

CHAPTER ONE

WHEN TWO WORLDS COLLIDE

As Jim McKenzie plodded purposely down a field of green shoots of grass, in his mud stained wellingtons, he could not remember whether he was the seventh or eighth generation of shepherds. But of one thing he was sure. He was the Last Shepherd.

Ahead of him, ever alert, was his faithful tricolour border collie Jess, having done her morning's work, herding and cajoling flocks of sheep on the hills above the village of Corsack in Galloway, south west Scotland. It gave Jim great satisfaction that his outdoor life was one of silence, interrupted by the instructional whistle to Jess but maintained by the silent flight of the red kite in the vicinity. He was a man in his mid thirties who had no interest in the hedonistic lifestyles of many of his contemporaries but he did occasionally wonder if he would ever find himself sharing his life with a partner again. But if that were to be the case, it was unlikely that shepherding would attract a new generation. Times were changing. Jim made sure they did so as slowly as he could. Shepherding skills and instilled country understanding passed down through many generations were gifts not to be lost without a fight.

From an adjacent field the cross wires of a telescopic rifle focused on the shepherd's steps advancing to the country road. On the opposite side of the hill, farmer Bob, in his early seventies, stood reading his newspaper by his Land Rover. He was distracted by an approaching car which slowed down. The car stopped by him and he saw a young good looking girl was at the wheel. He perked up. She lowered the car window.

'Are ye lost lassie?' he enquired.

'I've come to pregnancy diagnoses some heifers for you,' she said.

'Are ye sure? I wis waiting fur the vet, a man called Joe.'

The young girl got out of the car. She wore a padded waistcoat, jeans and wellies. Her hair was tied back, secured by a tartan ribbon. She laughed.

'Sorry to disappoint you but I am Jo, I'm the new vet. I was sent by the practice. It will be a good experience of large beasts for me.'

'Are ye fit enough to dae this lass? You've got a lot o' heifers here tae P. D.'

Jo smiled at him. It would be better to show what she could do rather than stand and argue about how the weaker sex were taking over in so many professions from engineering on the factory floor to the pulpits of the Bishopric in the Anglican church. She walked over to the barn and entered. She donned farm leggings and a heavy working jacket. Bob looked on impressed. She certainly seemed to know what she was about. Jo entered the rear of the cattle crush and stood beside a heifer. She lifted up its tail and entered the beast which showed no sign of discomfort.

'This one's in calf,' she called to Bob. She inspected the whole heard then passed them through a cattle race. She had a stick to prod them along. As each one passed, she inspected for any infestation, cuts, abrasions or any significant hoof injuries.

Bob laughed quietly and shook his head.

' I've underestimated yer capabilities.'

Jo smiled at him. She knew she had performed thoroughly. She turned on a hose and washed down her work overalls. But Bob took the hose from her and sprayed her feet.

They left the pen and returned to the roadside where on one leg Jo struggled out of her leggings. As she did, a new black Range Rover passed by, at high speed. It splashed both Bob and Jo with the muddy water. Jo gave a squeal. Bob let fly in a more masculine outburst.

'Ya bastard. What the hell do ye think yer dain?' But the driver did not slow down nor acknowledge his thoughtless driving.

On the other side of the hill, Jim was lambing a ewe near a stone dyke by the road. Jess sat motionlessly beside him watching the birth. The lamb emerged. Jim smiled at the new life, satisfied with another uncomplicated delivery. He cleaned it and set it on its feet shakily, returning it to its mother. As he did so the misty rain began to fall more heavily. Jim walked towards the gate by the road. He opened it and called Jess to go through and instructed her to sit on the other side. Obediently, as she had done many times before,

Jess sat on the edge of the road waiting for his master's next command. Jim closed the gate and bent down to pick up his crook.

The Land Rover approached at great speed. The driver suddenly applied his brakes and as the rubber burned the damp road, the noise of screeching alerted the neighbourhood. Jim looked round from his kneeling position. With a sharp yelp of pain Jess was hit by the car and was thrown under the vehicle. The car breaked, its velocity carrying it forward to off-balance Jim. He was propelled forward and collapsed. He lay semi conscious. He had swallowed his tongue.

The car pulled up and a braw well dressed man in his late forties, maybe early fifties, approached Jim from his new Range Rover. His children remained in the vehicle. His wife joined him. He saw Jim lying by the gate.

'Looks like a vagrant, a tramp,' he says disparagingly.

'Yes but darling, the dog, what about the poor dog? said Suzanne.

'These stray dogs are two a penny', he said dismissively.

Bob and Jo were standing on the other side of the hill by the cattle pen. Bob had made a mug of tea and they relaxed after the session in the barn with the heifers.

From a distant branch a rifle is made secure. The cross wires now focus on the tea drinkers. The trigger is gently squeezed. The shot cracked through the air. It landed between Jo and Bob.

'What was that?' asks Jo.

'It was a bullet,' Bob replied.

'Someone's trying to kill us.'

'No Jo. If he wis tryin tae kill us, we widna be standin' noo. We widnae hae heard the bang.'

No sooner had he spoken when a loud bang is heard. Bob scanned the horizon. He saw the marksman. He raised his arm and waved, acknowledging him.

'It's Tam, Big Tam. Thir must be somethin' rang. Cum on get intae the car.'

Bob commandeered Jo's Sabaru Impretza. Jo can find no words or reason to resist his sudden impulse. Instinctively she trusted him. He pulled back the seat to give himself leg room. Jo sat beside him.

'Ah ken the roads lass,' said Bob in a statement justifying his actions.

As they set off, Tam a broad built man of superb physical fitness, dressed in army camouflage ran down the field at full pelt. He leapt over a dyke on to the road in full view of the accident. He drew his dagger as he raced along the road. The ski mask which he wears only reveals one eye. He looks a sinister individual and Rupert's children Victoria and Edward scream in unison while hitting the window to attract their parents' attention.

'Look out behind you Dad!'

Their parents turned and saw the masked man with a high powered rifle slung over his back, clutching a long curved combat knife in his right hand. He barged between the couple. He knelt on one knee beside the unconscious Jim. Tam opened his mouth and was about to insert his knife when Rupert grabbed his arm. Tam threw his arm out aggressively and elbowed Rupert on the chin in a powerful punch which sent Rupert sprawling over his Range Rover.

'To hell with this madness. Let's get out of here. Come on, in the car quick,' Rupert ordered.

The Range Rover set off once more at speed while Tam carefully removed Jim's tongue from the back of his throat with his knife. Jim gasped for a breath of fresh air then was violently sick at the side of the road where he lay. Tam supported him in his state of shock.

Jo's car arrived at the scene and Bob and Jo got out promptly to see what had happened.

'You all right Jim?'

Jim came to his senses slowly and recognised Bob.

'What the hell's happened Bob? Where's Jess?'

'Come, let's get you to the warmth of my surgery. I'll call for an ambulance to take you to hospital,' said Jo.

'Tae hospital in Dumfries? Thirty miles away? No way. But a cup o tea will just be fine. So...you're the young vet?

'Aye, I am that and you know a vet is trained to work on animals, not folk like you Jim.'

'Och just patch me up as you would ony beast, lassie.'

Jo smiled at Jim. It was not the time to tell him about Jess's injuries. But there was something in Jim's determination which Jo rather liked.

Jo resumed the wheel to drive cautiously yet as fast as she could, to get Jim to her surgery. She drove without saying a word, nor did Bob or Tam who sat crouched in the rear of the car, anxiously aware of the condition of her injured passenger. She reversed to the back door of the surgery. Gently, Bob and Tam helped her to carry Jim inside where she laid Jim out on an operating table.

'You'll probably need an X–ray. But let me have a look at you first.'

She cut away his trousers with shears and opened his shirt. She could see some bruising where he had made contact with the rail. She then looked at his leg.

'He'll nae be wearin' they claes again', said Bob.

'That leg will need a couple of stitches and a good clean up. That must have been where the bumper caught you. Come on lads, let's get him to the X-ray table.'

Bob and Tam lay Jim out on the table and are told to stand well clear while the X-ray is taken. Jo attended to the X-ray in a side room while Bob approached Tam.

'Tam, we wis telt ye were killed in Afghanistan!' Tam did not respond. Instead he knelt over and collapsed to the clinic floor. Jo ran in from the ante room. Bob looked at Jo then Jim on his table and Tam on the floor.

'Thir must be sumthin' seriously wrang wi' him,' said Bob.

There was no need for Jo to reply. Action was what was required. Tam was placed on the operating table recently vacated by Jim. His ski mask was removed. His head was heavily bandaged on the right side of his face. It was blood stained and dirty. Bob assisted Jo in turning him over. There, they found blood stains on his back near a hole in his shirt, the size of a bullet. They removed his shirt and saw the bullet hole, surrounded by wheals and lash marks on his back causing infection. Jo examined the wounds carefully, dabbing disinfectant cotton wool as she did.

'This is not good. Tam will have to get to hospital', she said.

'He canna go tae hospital,' said Bob

'Why ever not?' asked Jo incredulously.

'We've been telt he wis killed in action in Afghanistan but as ye can see, he's somewhat alive here in oor patch.'

'Not as alive as we would hope for. What was he out there for, do you know?'

'It wis the army. The Royal Engineers in fact. He wis drilling bore holes for water supplies.'

'But I don't understand. Why is he supposed to be dead?'

Bob looked at Jo. He shook his head.

'We jist don't know what happened oot there. That's for sure. It may be that the Authorities that wis tryin tae get rid o him; aye even kill him but as I said, we really don't know. An' he canna tell us.'

Jo thought for a moment. No patient ever complained of her surgery skills but perhaps that is why she chose veterinary surgery. Then she recalled that Professor David Purley had awarded her the Starmer award for veterinary surgery in her final year, only two years ago. That gave her the necessary encouragement. She scrubbed her hands. She sterilized the implements required and prepared Tam for surgery.

Jo eased a bullet from his shoulder and placed it in a kidney bowl. She cleansed the wound and covered it with gauze. She then slowly undid his head bandage and was horrified to find he had only one eye. Clearly a bullet had entered his eye, travelled through the roof of his mouth, permanently damaging his tongue and rendered him speechless. She saw where the bullet had left though his cheek. No wonder he covered such a face disfiguring wound; what an amazing wonder he was still alive, she felt.

'We really should get him to hospital', Jo said in a whisper.

'We canna. Simply canna', said Jim.

'Jim's right. Keep him here jist noo and do as much as ye can', said Bob.

Jo took his temperature.

'It's 105 degrees. I'll have to give him penicillin. I can only hope he won't react to it. This is meant for animals you realise, but in the circumstances, it will have to do.'

Jo gave him the penicillin and tried to make him comfortable. She raised the metal rail around the mattress and left him to sleep. It was a deep sleep but Jo rarely took her eyes off her second human patient.

CHAPTER TWO

THE CRANNOG SERVES.

At the heart of this small community was the village pub. The Crannog had been serving locals and passersby for more than one hundred and fifty years. In the days when the Kirk was in the ascendency, the takings were down but now the Crannog offered itself as a responsible drinking venue which rarely saw any trouble. It only heard of troubles. Family troubles, local affairs of the heart, on goings of local business and any gossip worth repeating was fodder for the bar.

Jim had recovered sufficiently to gain movement and his legs were more than willing to return to his local pub. Jock Doig, the owner was already serving at the bar when they arrived.

'So whit have ye been up to the night?' he asked.

Jo, Jim and Bob began to speak simultaneously. Jock raised his hand.

'Wheesht, one o' ye at a time, please'.

'I've never kent a day like it in all o' ma years' said Bob.

'Aye, an' I thought I wis a gonner,' said Jim.

'Tae think nothin' ever goes on in this wee place!' laughed Bob.

Jock noticed Jim's bandaged leg.

'Good grief. What's Jim been dain? Did a heifer have a go at him?'

Bob leant over the bar and in a lowered voice told Jock what events had taken place over the past day. Jim did not have to relive his horrors. He was seated beside Jo at a table by the fire, nursing a pint of bitter. Jo sipped her bitter too. But being aware that she may have to nurse Tam on her return, her bitter was lemon.

In a nearby holiday home Rupert and his wife Suzzane were also recalling the recent events. Their tempers were raised as Rupert tried to justify his behaviour.

'We should have stopped to help that man,' said Suzzane.

'What! With a crazy gunman with a dagger nearby? Anyway that man is probably dead by now. Killed by the gunman I am sure. We could not have done anything to help. In fact you can thank me for getting you all away from there as fast as I could'.

His daughter Victoria took up the challenge to his authority.

'But what about the poor dog, Daddy?'

Her question floated unanswered as Rupert vented his anger at his wife.

'It's all your fault Suzzane. If you had only read the map properly, we would not have got in this situation.'

Suzzane had had enough. There was only one way to resolve the argument. The police had to catch this local maniac. She took her mobile 'phone from her handbag and dialled 999. She walked around the room then passed by the window trying to get a signal. Victoria tried her mobile telephone and not to be left out Rupert dialled 999 too on his expensive blackberry.

'God Almighty. Cut off from the real world with a mad gunman on the loose,' he said.

Edward came down from his bedroom wired to sound. He took out his earpiece.

'What's up? What are you all doing?' he asked.

Suzzane replied that they could not get a signal to telephone.

'Forget mobiles, use the house phone. They must have one. Or maybe they use pigeon post up here?' Edward laughed at his own joke.

They searched the house for a telephone cable or a phone but the system had been withdrawn.

'I saw a red telephone box in the village near the pub. You could use that I suppose', said Edward.

Back at the pub, Jock had heard the full story and was amazed to hear what had happened. After a second round, Jo decided to return home to check on Tam. Bob and Jim nod their agreement and promised to return soon. As Jo left the pub and walked near to her car, she heard a whimper. She saw Jess wagging her tail but clearly in discomfort. She bent down and stretched her hand towards her. She could see that Jess was in real distress so she gathered the dog carefully and placed her on the front seat of her car.

She drove back to the surgery and carried Jess into her office.

When she got there, the surgery was fully lit. She placed Jess on her operating table and looked around each room. But Tam was no longer there. He must have discharged himself! She shook her head. The thought passed her mind that if Tam was found dead by the roadside, what questions would be asked of her as a vet, for treating a patient who should have been hospitalised? The thought disturbed her.

Jo settled down to work on Jess. The dog took kindly to her and then she was placed under sedation. It was a long operation with no assistance. Swabs and medications multiply by the table. Jo gave Jess as much of a fighting chance as she could. The prospect of amputation loomed large in her mind. That brought her thoughts to the difference between a three legged family pet and a three legged working collie. The fate of each could not be so cruelly different.

When Bob and Jim left the pub an hour later, they noticed their transport had been taken by Jo. Quick thinking Bob saw his neighbour's pickup outside Jock's shop. He knocked on the door and George opened it.

'Just as well I've no been drinkin' boys. Guess ye want a lift home? You look a sorry sight,' said George. 'In ye get.'

Jim tried to get into the back seat. He cannot bend his sore leg easily. Bob gave him a hand. Naturally George is concerned and on the mile home, he heard of the events which led to his injury. George returned home as Bob remembered he still had the heifers in a pen.

'Give me a minute Jim, I'll hae tae release they heifers.'

After they have all been released, Bob returned to his Land Rover. Jim was already inside.

'It's been a long day. Let's call it off now'.

Bob drove Jim to his house and helped him out of the car.

'Will ye be a'right then Jim?'

'Aye, Aye I will. Thanks Bob'.

On his own again Jim struck a match to light a candle. He carried the candle through to the kitchen and poured himself a glass of Walkers's Red Label whisky. He added three drops of water. He sat down by a dying fire and reminisced. He looked up at the photo on the mantelpiece, of his late wife, Mary. Then he looked at the empty basket by his side.

'You were taken fae me first Mary. And noo you too, Jess.'

He took a final swig of his drink, blew out the candle and wrapped a blanket over himself. His melancholy did not last long. The drink had defeated him. His snoring could lift the rafters.

CHAPTER THREE

BUSY LINES

Early next day when a heavy early mist gradually rose, leaving vapour trails as mystical as the tail of Tam O'Shanter's mare, Jim woke. He raised himself from his fireside chair and grimaced at the pain still felt in his injured leg. He staggered towards the door where a brush was propped up. He used it as a makeshift crutch and made his way to the kitchen to make some toast and a cup of tea. By the time he had eaten and washed up, it was much lighter. He opened the door and somewhat unsteadily approached a small tractor with a transport box attached. He sparked the engine into life.

His tractor entered a field in search of any overnight lamb deliveries. He came to the brow of the field and stopped. He applied the brakes. He scoured the land to see if any sheep was giving birth in seclusion. On turning round he saw Bob's Land Rover had entered the field and was approaching him. Jim dismounted the tractor and awaited his arrival.

'Ye can't walk wi a leg like that!'

'I've never missed checkin' the sheep in twenty years an' am no aboot tae gee up noo.'

Jim determinedly showed his ability to use his crutch but after a few steps, the make shift crutch sank into the soft earth and broke. Jim lost his balance and fell to the ground rolling in agony. Bob ran after him and picked him up.

'C'mon Jim lad, let's get ye home'.

'Bit whit aboot the ewes? They're oot there burstin' tae lamb and thirs nayone tae see ower them.'

'Aye but it'll nae be you in this state'.

'Thirs nae one else, Bob. Jist nae one at a'.'

Tam appeared from almost nowhere to join the argument but gestured that he can oversee the lambing in the fields. Bob smiled.

'That's the best offer yet an' I can always gie him ony advice he might need,' said Bob.

Bob led Jim to his Land Rover and they took him home again. But as they entered the courtyard they saw Jo's car was already there. Jo came over to greet them and Jim lowered his window.

'How are you feeling today, Jim?'

'I feel like havin' been run over by a Range Rover.'

'Well I've got a surprise for you.'

'Fur me?'

Jo walked back to her car, opened the back door which caused Jim to see what the surprise was.

'Jess! Ma wee darling.'

Jess managed to wag her tail while Jo carried Jess into the house. Bob gave Jim a hand back to his house.

Jo placed Jess down on the carpet.

'Ma wee Jess. Yiv lost yer leg!

Jess limped over to her favourite corner of the room, wagging her tail but devoid of her usual alertness.

Jim gazed at the companion that once was his workmate. It filled him wi' drool.

'Bob, she'll nae be able tae work onymair. Gie her tae Tam and get him tae shoot her.'

'No way! said Jo. 'I've spent three hours in surgery with Jess last night and you want to put her down?'

Bob and Jim look guiltily at each other.'Ok, ok, Jo. Ok' said Jim.

'What is it with you lot since I came here? We have a male chauvinist pig over there,' she pointed at Bob. Then pointing at Jim, 'a stubborn and ungrateful one here who doesn't know when he's hurt and hell bent on murdering Jess, his best friend! Not to mention a one eyed apparent psychopath who takes pot shots at me in the middle of no-where.'

Naturally there was a deadly hush after Jo's outburst as each contemplated how they had tarnished their images. Jim knew how to resolve the atmosphere.

'Would ye like a cup o tea, Jo?' She smiled at Jim. 'Two sugars and no milk.'

'What nae milk! Remember I'm a dairy farmer!' said Bob.

'We can't all be perfect!'

Bob went through to make the tea but stopped to pat Jess on his way through. Jess's tail throbbed and her kindly eyes looked at her master's unusually lame stance. Bob found the caddy and brewed a strong cup, made palatable by the Glengarry biscuits he found in the biscuit tin.

'Jim, hope you don't mind me open the Glengarries.'
'Glengarry biscuits? I didna ken I had ony.'

He looked at Jo. She raised her hand. 'I've a lot tae thank ye for Jo. You've done a good job on Jess and yer right, I'd be lost wi' oot her. And for lookin' after me and no jist wi these biscuits!

'Come here Jim. Let me have another look at your leg.'

She unbound the bandage and cleaned his leg with warm water and soap. She dried it gently patting it as Jim held his breath and then she placed a new bandage in place.

'I'll have to do this regularly. That is if you don't mind me seeing you without your trousers on!'

'I've nae modesty left ma dear but I need someone to help Tam till I'm ready tae get back oot tae the fields. I canny expect Tam tae do it a' himself.'

Bob was in a reflective mood sipping his tea. His eyes suddenly lit up.

'Hey, I've got a plan tae sort yer problems oot!'
'What! Ye must be jokin''said Jim.
'Trust me. I've a plan o' richt'

At Rupert and Suzanne's holiday house Rupert is admiring the view from the lounge window.

'Suzzane, come and see the view right up the glen. It's much clearer this morning.'

Suzzane glanced out of the window but is distracted by her mobile telephone lying on the sofa. She checks to see if she has a text message. Rupert does the same with his blackberry.

'Let's go down to the village to see if there has been an arrest yet and we can use the telephone there. Ok get the kids up, let's go'.

'Were on holiday remember Rupert. Let them lie in a bit. It's Easter for heaven's sake'.

Two hours later with the family all on board, Rupert pulled up by the old red telephone box. He got out of the car and entered the kiosk. There was no telephone in the kiosk. He returned to his car and drove down to Jock's local cum postal shop. His assistant Sally, a mother of three children under ten years of age, was behind the counter.

'Can I help you sir?' she says.

'I need to make a telephone call'.

'Are you looking for a pay phone?'

'Yes. Damn poor reception on my mobile.'

'Well, there's one in the pub. Except the pub's not open yet. You could try the garage.'

'Where's that then?'

'It's Jock's garage, just a wee bit along from the pub. He'll be there.'

'Good heavens. So what does Jock not own and run in the village?'

'Well, there's the Police station and the Kirk. He doesn't own them.'

Rupert left without a word of thanks and got into his car once more. He drove along the 200 metres to Jock's garage and parked alongside.

Jock was aware of his arrival but remained under the car he was working on, with his legs protruding out. Rupert coughs to attract attention.

'Hullo, can I do anything fur ye?'

'Have you got a pay phone?'

'A pay phone? Aye, I've got a pay phone.'

'Can I use it?' asked Rupert.

'No. It's not workin' It broke last week and BT

haven't been round tae fix it yet. I keep speakin' tae some wan in India. They say they canny understand me, an' tae be frank the feeling's mutual. Onyway, they say they're testin' the line.' Nothin' I can do till then. Jock pulled himself out from under the car. He looked over at Rupert's car. He wiped his hands on his overalls.

'Oh that's one o' they up-market sports Range Rovers. Worth a bonny penny. Mind if I have a look at it?'

Rupert is particularly proud of his car. He gestured to him to have a look around his car. Jock saw the family sitting in the car. He smiled at them as he ran his hand along the body work. He went round to the front of the car and found a piece of the grill broken. He pulled out some muddy jacket cloth from the damaged car.

'Ah see yiv hit something.'

'Er ....we hit a small deer a few miles back down the road,' he lied.

'And was the deer wearing a jacket by ony chance?'

'No,....I...er...caught my jacket on it,' his lies got thicker.

'Oh, I see, ... I think I see'.

'What about the telephone. What should I do?'

'The pub will open at 6pm. You'll get it then.'

'And will the pub phone be working?'

'Oh aye, it will be working jist fine I assure you. So we'll see you later?'

Rupert returned to his car somewhat disgruntled. As his car set off, the telephone in the garage rang. Jock smiled with relief that it did not ring when Rupert was present.

'Hello, Jock here.'

'Hi Jock, it's Bob.'

'I wis jist aboot tae phone ye. Ye ken that Range Rover wi' the posh guy an' his family?

'Aye I certainly do. What aboot them?'

'Well he's just been here and he didn't let oot onythin aboot the accident. Told me he hit a deer. The funny thing bein' that the deer must hae been wearing Jim's jacket! Anyway, he'll be back at the pub at 6pm when it opens. He needs to make a call. '

'Good news to ma ears. Well here's what we'll do. I think it's time we gave him a reception party. After all, he's on holiday isn't he?'

Bob laughed uncontrollably and infectiously. Jock joined in too. He was not entirely sure of what Bob had in mind but it was something that was clearly to his liking.

It is opening time at The Crannog and the bar is full almost as soon as the hour of six struck. Word has got out that something is in the air, there is even a crousie atmosphere around but no one except Jock and Bob are in the know. The speculation caused a real hubbub of expectation and it's a noisy place until the door opened and Rupert entered to make his call. The pub fell silent and all eyes were on the holidaymaker. Sarcasm fights to leave Bob's lips.

'It won't be easy making a telephone call in this place. Anyway, I thought you had not got a telephone in these parts.'

An old man turned in his chair and turned on Rupert.

'No phone! I remind ye sir, it wis the Scots who invented the telephone, Sir Alexander Tingaling Bell in fact!'

Rupert ignored the jibe and proceeded to the bar. Jock offered him the telephone and he made his call. The noise returned to the bar and Rupert is forced to cover his exposed ear. Through necessity he made his call brief. Jock noticed the phone call had terminated so offered Rupert a drink.

'What will ye be havin', mister? I did nae catch yer name.'

'It's Rupert, Rupert Parker Smythe.'

'Rupert Parker Smith, a fine name ye have there.'

'The Smythe is spelled with a Y and an E'.

'Of course Rupert, of course. So what will it be then?

'A small whisky please.'

As Jock poured the drink, Jim approached the bar and took up a stance beside Rupert looking at him, curiously. Rupert felt an uncomfortable interest being shown in him.

'I think I know you. Seen you somewhere before, I think?'

'So what do you do for a livin' Mr Parker-Smythe?'

'I work in the city.'

'An' what do you do in the city?' asked Jim.

'I'm a successful Hedge Fund Banker, actually.'

'I work wi' hedges too, you might say!'

'Really?'

'Ay' I'm Jim McKenzie. I live at Bengatton Farm.'

'He's the Last Shepherd,' said the old man nursing his half pint.

'The Last Shepherd. Why are you called that?'

'Because I'm the only one left in the glen who still farms wi' a dog an' a stick, the auld way. So tell me how much does a Hedge Banker earn?

'To give you an idea, my Christmas bonus last year was three million pounds. Others actually did better but I was quite well paid.'

'That's a lot o' money. ...Do you think if I locked ye up in a shipping container wi' yer £3m you could survive by eatin it,' Mr Parker Smythe?'

'Whatever do you mean?'

'Well, I'm sayin' if ye had a' the money an' nae food, then ye really have nuthin'.

'I'd find a supermarket somewhere.'

'But that's no whir food comes fae'.

'It's where we get ours. So where do you think it comes from?'

'How much do ye think ye rely on a farmer?'

'Oh not much these days. Farming is a dying business I'd say.'

'A lot mair than you obviously think Mr Parker Smythe. Look, yer wearing a pair o' leather shoes. Where did they come fae?'

'A shoe shop of course.'

'Aye a shoe shop, How silly o' me. But where did the shop get the shoes? The leather comes fae coos ye ken! Yer woolly socks come fae the sheep on the hills. The farmer gets up early and brings the sheep to get clipped; then we sell the fleece but it doesnae pay for the clippen' o' them.'

'But that can't be right,' said Rupert.

'Aye, but that's the way it is.'

Rupert gave thought to this exchange while he took another sip of his single malt. Jim took advantage to humiliate his foe.

'I see ye like yer whisky.'

'I can certainly tell a good one. Years of experience one might say. Jolly good one this McAllan.'

'Aye, but the farmer had tae plough the field then sow the barley. After that he worried for six months. Will the barley grow? Will he get a good price for it? An' ye don't think ye rely on the farmer? I tell you Mr Parker-Smythe, you widnae enjoy your quality o' life without the farmer. Ye see ma freend, we're nae tramps and vagrants.'

The words haunt Rupert. 'Tramps and vagrants'. He suddenly realises who he has been speaking to. He turned to leave the pub as this confrontation has become increasingly confrontational. As he is about to leave the pub he is glad to see his family grouped together but they look apprehensive as they are accompanied by a police officer. Rupert saw the fire door on the adjacent wall. As he walked smartly to this exit, he opened the door to find a man standing in his way. He was a masked man.

Tam lifted his arm and struck Rupert across the chest sending Rupert back through the fire door. He crashed to the ground and was soon apprehended by PC Sandy Dunn.

'Mr Rupert Parker Smythe I am arresting you. You do not have to say anything now but if you do, it will be recorded and may be used at a later date at your trial. Do you understand?'

'Officer I hear what you say but this is ridiculous, you have no grounds to detain me.'

'Leaving the scene of an accident and not reporting it? Failing to assist an injured person and I think after your abrupt exit from the fire door, that constitutes resisting arrest. I make that three charges, do you?'

As PC Dunn took Rupert into custody, Suzanne tried to intervene.

'Please let him go, he has not done anything. He's innocent I assure you.'

'Please madam, back off. Look after your children, and I'll look after your husband.'

Victoria and Edward cannot understand the sudden developments and the legal proceedings as Suzanne drove them to their house. Meanwhile at the police station as PC Dunn filled out his arrest form, Rupert has his own agenda to clarify.

'So, what about the maniac with the gun? That man in the mask who threw me out of the fire door?'

'Maniac? Did you say maniac? I didn't see any maniac, sir.' PC Dunn replied.

Rupert thought long and hard. It seemed the community was against him and now the conveniently blind officer, who turned a blind eye to the masked man, seemed to be the final straw to brake the camel's back. He could play by their rules too.

'Officer I see the game. Turning the blind eye when it is appropriate to do so. Good policy. Well, I can make it very much more comfortable for you financially, if you know what I mean?'

'And how would that be sir?' asked PC Dunn naively but setting a trap.

'You know money. A thousand; perhaps two if you agree?'

'And would that be what one calls a bribe?'

'Just a couple of thousand to let me go, officer. Nobody would know.'

'Nobody will know Mr Parker-Smythe because I never heard your offer. Now, home address, age and of course full name please. You might wish to think these replies carefully while I lead you through to the cell.'

PC Dunn locked Rupert in the cell.

'Three thousand?'

'No, no, no.'

'Five thousand. That's my final offer. Come on what do you say to that? I promise I can get it to you by tomorrow afternoon.'

'A little deaf are you Mr Smythe? You will be at court at 10am tomorrow morning. In the meantime I'm considering adding the bribery charge, yes attempting to bribe a police officer on duty, mmm...very serious indeed. Now that carries quite a sentence on its own!'

CHAPTER FOUR

COURTING TROUBLE

Rupert woke in his cell the next morning and realised where he was. He stood at the cell door and bawled out.

'Let me out, do you hear? Let me out.'

'Wheesht, wheesht, yer croudie-time will be ready in a few minutes. What do you take in yer tea?'

'You can do a lot with £5,000. That's a fair subsidy on your salary I'm sure.'

'Now don't be silly Mr ummm Parker-Smythe. And any more bribery taunts and I promise you will be charged with that too.'

PC Dunn brought a tray with his breakfast on it and placed it on a table outside the cell. He drew two chairs up to it. Then unlocked Rupert and brought him to the table.

'Now just to let you know the procedure, there will be

a hearing before the Justices of the Peace in the village hall. '

'My lawyer will be here by 10am.'

'That's fine. We'll wait for him.'

'And what will happen at the hearing?'

'Well, they have to decide whether the case should go to the Sheriff court or not.'

'Why should they be involved?'

'It might give you a better chance to clear your name.'

'Ah well, I am sure they'll clear me.'

PC Dunn left Rupert to finish his meal in peace.

Three hours later PC Sandy Dunn escorted Rupert into the Village Hall. As they approached, a smart executive saloon car pulled up. A disgruntled lawyer gets out of the car. He entered the hall and approached Rupert.

'Rupert Parker Smyth. Do you realise I have been driving for seven hours this morning to defend you? Make sure your next holiday is near an airport if you wish my services again!'

Mr Mark Skelling LL.B (Hons.) (Cantab.) engaged in an animated whispered discussion with Rupert as they sat at the long wooden table with twisted treacle legs. The Chairman of the Justices arrived together with his two other justices. They all rise. Rupert puts his face in his hands as he sees the Chair of the Justices is the local garage, shop and bar manager, Jock!

'Gentlemen, please be seated' says Jock.

All present return to their seats except for an animated Mark Skelling, who antagonised the bench.

'These proceedings are a farce.'

'I take it you appear for Mr Rupert Parker Smythe? Your name and qualifications please?'

Indeed I do. Mr Mark Skelling LL,B. Honours Cambridge University. Of Skelling and Skelling, Solicitors, Farnham, Surrey.'

'Let me remind you Mr Skelling, you are no longer in England. Scots law differs...considerably. Today's procedures are preliminary by nature. Sui generis you will recognise and understand?'

Mr Skelling sat down and folded his arms and huffed.

'Mr Rupert Parker-Smyth, please stand.'

'It is alleged that you were involved in a hit and run accident; failing to stop after the accident; failing to report the said accident, and finally, an even more serious charge of attempting to bribe a police officer.'

What Rupert does not know is that Justice Jock is reading from memory. It is a blank paper he is holding. He places it down on the table.

'These are serious allegations Mr Parker Smythe. Normally at this point we have to consider whether it is a case for the Sheriff court or not. However as you might find and be enlightened Mr Skilling, Scots law can be flexible...if not canny!'

'Canny? Mr Justice', asked Mr Skelling.

'Aye canny. Mr Skelling. Fortunate...that's canny.'

Mr Skelling looked puzzled and conveyed his demeanour to Rupert.

'You see I propose another solution.'

Mr Skelling threw his open palms in the air. He haunched his shoulders and awaited the tribunal's decision.

'The man you knocked down Mr Parker Smythe, simply can't do his lambing as a result of this accident. But if you would do his lambing for the next two weeks, then these charges before you will be dropped.'

Jock gave Rupert and his solicitor a moment to consider his proposal. In an animated discussion Rupert still maintained his innocence but Mark felt it would be well nigh impossible to defend some of the charges and the bribery charge was particularly worrying. Their discussion was not heard by all until in exasperation Mark told Rupert:

'For God's sake take the deal. It will keep your record clean.'

Hesitatingly and indeed grudgingly, Rupert held back his pride and agreed to the offer. Mark was quick to his feat before his client changed his mind.

'My client accepts the conditions on the understanding that the charges he is currently facing, all of them, will be struck off, wiped permanently off the record.'

'My word is my word. Thou's get the Saul o boot!'

'Your meaning sir?'

'It's Burns, Mr Skelling. I put my soul into the bargain. Now be off wi' ye and count yourself lucky.'

The meeting ended and all rose as the Justices left the village hall. Mr Skelling turned towards Rupert and shook his hand.

'My legal fees and my travel expenses will be sent to your home address by the end of the month. Now for that long drive home. And at least an hour's drive before the motorway. Happy Easter, Mr Parker Smythe.'

Mark Skelling drove off having exchanged his pin-striped dark suited jacket for his favourite Belfry golf jersey with the years 2003-4 Club Captain embossed over his heart. With his sun glasses perched on his nose, he opened the window to enjoy the fresh air and count the amassing fees he obtained for his twenty four hours work in a Scottish Justice court. In the back of his car, he heard the jangle of his golf clubs. The day was sunny and as he passed through Dumfries on the Edinburgh Road, he spotted the Dumfries County Golf Club by the river Nith. He could not resist. He delayed his return home by three and a half hours. In that time he lost two balls to the Nith, achieved three birdies; twelve pars and three bogies which he put down to being not used to having played the course.

Earlier in the day, Rupert returned to his car where his wife and children had been awaiting the result of his court appearance. They were delighted to see him return apparently, a free man.

'They dropped the charges. But they did so on one condition. I have to spend the next two weeks lambing for the shepherd I knocked down.'

'That's wonderful news darling', said Suzzane.

'You mean you are not going to prison after all?' said Victoria. 'Mum said that you might be going to prison.'

Rupert laughed.

'Treat it as a real holiday Rupert. Or a new experience, away from telephones and big money deals. It will be a great story for our dinner parties. You might even find it relaxing.'

'Yea Dad, it is better than a prison sentence any day, with all the murderers and thieves.'

They laugh at the children's lively imaginations and return to their house.

Later that morning Jo drove to Jim's house and pulled up by his front door.

'It's Jo the vet. I've come to change your dressing.'

As she is about to knock on the door, the door opened with a flourish. It's Tam who opens the door in Jim's house.

I'm here to change Jim's dressing and your's too Tam. I've got the pair of you to attend to.'

She entered the kitchen where she found Jim stretched out asleep with Jess on his lap. Jim, came round bleary eyed and Jess hobbled off his lap.

'I said I've come to change your dressing', said Jo.

'Ah, it's you ma dear. Ok, I'm a willing patient.'

Jo starts to unwind a bandage when she glimpses a photo on his mantelpiece.

'So, are you a married man Jim?'

'Er..aye.'

So where's your wife then?'

'She's no longer with me, she left me last year,' he says.

'Oh I'm sorry to hear that.'

'Aye, it's a shame...but I'm all right.'

'Will she be coming back then Jim?'

'No, she'll no be back. She canna.'

Jo continued to tend Jim's leg when Bob and Jock arrived.

'Good news Jim, Guess what we've done? We've got yon city bloke to dae yer lambing,' said Jock.

'I'll show him the ropes for a couple o' days,' said Bob.

'Ye must be kiddin'. He'll nae ken one end o' a sheep fae the aither. An' he widna ken if it wis lambin' even if it came up an' bit him on the arse!'

They all laugh.

'Steady Jim, I'm not finished with this bandage. I think I can fix yer wounds but not yer language, it seems.'

'Think we'd better be on oor way, best tae keep oot o' the nurse's way. See you soon Jim.'

'Oh and oan your way out tell Tam, I'll be ready for him in a minute, to change his dressing.'

'Tell Tam? I havnae seen Tam the day.'

Jo looks at Jim then Bob.

'But Tam let me in only five minutes ago and I told him I'd be seeing to him after Jim.'

'Naw, we didn't see him when we arrived.'

'Tams's his ain man. You'll catch up wi' him before long. Tyin' him doon's anaither thing I guess, said Jock.

CHAPTER FIVE

NAILED TO THE TASK

Early the next day at 7.40am, Rupert with the entire family, drove up to Jim's farmyard at Bengatton in his Range Rover. Jim, Bob and Jock were all there to welcome them.

'All present and correct sirs. Well, what do you wish us all to do?' said Rupert enthusiastically.

'I see you've got the whole family involved. Is that what you all want to do?' asked Jock.

'It should be an educational experience in the fresh air. We certainly wish to be involved,' said Suzzane.

'Aye educational and bloody hard work too. You'll be startin' wi' me up on the hill an' I'll show yous what tae dae. But first yer nae gaun in they claes! Come on go an' get changed,' requested Bob.

They had arrived with a wardrobe of clothes in their

car. A surplus of boots, waterproofs and Gortex body-warmers were brought in from the boot. The family swapped and changed clothing items until they felt somewhat comfortable then reported once more for duty. Bob lead them up through a field and to a gate where he stopped to address them once more.

'Noo, sheep are silly but no daft. They are no alwis co-operative. Jist like some humans eh?'

Not waiting for an answer Bob set off again but Suzzane and the children are bogged down in mud by the gate. Victoria slipped headfirst into the mud, rising with a muddy face. Suzzane lost a welly and her balance while Rupert struggled to keep pace with Bob and started to become breathless.

'Noo this is where the collies come in useful, ye see....'

Bob turned round to see how far back the family were.

'Fur f...goodness sake, it's gonna be a long day.'

Rupert eventually caught up on Bob breathing heavily.

'So, where are the sheep?' he asks.

'We've got tae find the sheep. They dinna come lookin' fur us.'

'But there's nothing here!'

'We've jist started man. There's anaither three miles ahead o' us.'

'What another three miles?'

'An' tae think. Jail seems a far warmer restful place to be, don't ye think?'

Rupert took the hint and rallied round.

'Right then, let's find the sheep.'

'Don't forget yer family. Yid better wait fur them,' Bob said.

It takes another six minutes before a mud spattered family appear. When they meet up there is much panting and deep breaths of air.

'We've another three miles to go. Sorry,' said Rupert.

'Come on then. We'll be the fittest family when we finish and get back to Surrey,' said Suzanne.

Now walking in unison, they did not go far before Bob pointed out a sheep which has just given birth. They approach it, but keep their distance.

'We don't need tae dae onythin' tae this wan.'

Forty five minutes later they have walked another mile.

'How much longer?' asks a weary Rupert.

'Not until we've got the job done. Nut like walking the city streets o' London Toon is it?' teased Bob.

But the family seem to agree with Bob's assessment.

'Bob, I hope you don't mind me asking, but what age are you?'

'How old do yi think I am?'

'I'd say 56 or maybe 60?'

'72 last June', said Bob.

'You should have retired and have your feet up by the fire.'

'And why wid I dae that? Thirs nothin' like being ootdoors in the fresh air wi the skylark above.'

Bob turned to look Rupert straight in the eye.

'If I did nae hiv this, I'd hae nothin' tae live fur.'

They have now turned full circle and are back at Bengatton where there are some two hundred sheep in the pens. Jo, Jim and Tam are trimming the sheep's feet. The family watch as Tam turns a sheep and smartly trims its feet.

'Can we have a go at this?' asks Edward.

Tam motions Edward over to him. He shows Edward how to clip their feet.

Meanwhile Jo is working in a pen. She is with a ewe lambing. She turns to Suzzane.

'Would you like to lamb it?'

Suzzane smiled. She rolled up her sleeves. Jo caught a ewe and showed her what to do.

'We need to get two feet and a nose.'

Jo puts her hand into the ewe and brings out the other foot.

'The lamb will come out now. Suzzane you have a go at delivering it.'

'Oh super. I'd love to.'

'Wo, woe...you can't put your hands inside the sheep with those nails! You will cause damage to her. You'll have to trim those nails,' shouted Bob.

Tam overheard the conversation. He approached Suzzane with foot trimmers. He grabbed her outstretched hand and stepped over her arm so that it protruded between his legs. He started to cut her nails.

'My nails! Oh my God, my nails! They will take months to grow again.'

Suzzane saw her nail clippings drop into the mud.

'Just because you have no nails, you bastard,' she cries.

Jo continued with her lambing while Tam released Suzzane from his grip. She looked at her outstretched hands both shorn like a sheep. Jo can now let her deliver a lamb. But Rupert and the children are watching and they feel it's been a long day. Rupert announced that they will be back tomorrow after a good night's sleep, the fresh air had guaranteed that. They got into their car and set off back to their house.

'Well, that went well I jist canna say. It's no yet five

o'clock an' they're awa' hame. But we canna dae the lambin' wi nae one tae dae it,' said Jim.

'I've got cattle tae feed back at mine noo. Sorry, but I'll hiv tae be goan soon,' said Bob.

'So jist what can wi dae?' asks Jim.

'It would be better if the family were to live with you at the farm,' suggested Jo.

'I canna feed a' them, an'I dinnae hiv the money, let alain goan shoppin' cos o' ma leg,' said Jim.

Tam held one finger to the sky. He slung his rifle over his shoulder and started to run up the hill slowly disappearing in a mist.

'Where's Tam going Jim?' asked Jo

'I dinna ken but he's up tae sumthin' an' a don't think a like it.'

'Right let me take you back to the house.'

'We'll hae tae let the sheep oot first.'

It did not take Jo long to release the sheep. Once they started, they followed in rapid succession and that meant Jim did not have to wait long for his lift home.

Jo helped Jim out of her car at Jim's farm house. She enjoyed supporting him and relished life in her changing role from vet to nurse as it seemed.

'Now if you need me anytime, day or night, I'll be more than happy to come round. You know that, don't you?' she said.

Jim smiled at her kind thought.

'Thanks, thanks very much Jo'.

Jim's lingering gaze at Jo's face and the proximity to each other found Jim taking hold of Jo by both hands and bringing her forward. She did not resist. They smiled at each other. Then their lips met for the very first time. It was a magical moment for them both and led to a warm embrace.

CHAPTER SIX

GUDDLING IN WATER

Rupert and his family arrived at the house, hungry and tired. The children ran inside to get their personal sterios back on their lugs, while Suzzane wondered what meal would satisfy a worn out family. Unbeknown to them Tam stood crouched behind the house's privet hedge. He looked over the hedge just as Rupert, the last one to enter the house, turned to close the door behind him. It was a close call and Tam was disappointed in his timing. It flowed against his military training. He vowed to take even more precaution as he jumped over the hedge and took up a position by the drainpipe at the corner of the building. The walls were thick as in all traditional houses nevertheless Tam smiled when he heard Suzanne's wail penetrate the building.

'Why did you not stop that madman from cutting my nails?' But no response was forthcoming.

Tam put his rifle down on the grass beside the house. He shimmied up the drainpipe agilely taking a peep into the lounge as he did so. He saw Edward playing with a hand held video game. He climbed further up and saw that the bathroom was engaged. There was no misinterpreting what he saw and heard in the frosted window. Victoria was bent over the lavatory bowl with her fingers in her mouth. The lassie was trying to make herself sick.

Tam continued on to the roof of the house where he was able to prise open the Velux window on the roof with great care. He entered the attic stealthily like a cat on the prowl. Then he made a small hole in the flooring. This gave him sight of the feuding parents. He froze until they left their bedroom and returned downstairs.

Tam then placed his back against the header tank and his feet against a joist. He strained to push the tank. After several unsuccessful attempts, he saw it start to tip over. One more push and the water tank came off its rafters and broke through the attic floor into the bedroom. The tank could not be restrained. It crashed through the bedroom floor on to the lounge floor spilling gallons of water in its wake. Inevitably, all hell was let loose in the house with screaming commands to get outside to safety. They feared the house would fall down.

Rupert was first out of the door with a torrent of water following behind him. Edward was dumbstruck with his mouth as large as Kippford bay, holding on to his video game. Victoria ran out of the house into her mother's arms and Edward eventually found enough momentum to join the rest of the family outside. All members of the family were drenched and in shock.

Their response was to get into their car and head for

the village. When they set off, Tam was able to retrace his steps by returning to the roof to examine his disastrous plot. Then he slid down the down pipe, picked up his rifle, threw it over his shoulder and walked away.

The Parker Smythe's car arrived outside the pub. The four wet holidaymakers entered self consciously and wondered what kind of reception they might get.

'My Goad! What on earth has happened tae you all?' asked Jock.

'The roof fell in. The water tank is in the lounge. Water is everywhere. I thought a holiday house would have been more substantially built. It was a death trap. I tell you, a death trap. We are lucky to be alive,' declared Rupert.

'Aye, mighty dondie. What a disaster. At least you are all alive. That's one blessin'. Well, let me see. I've a room upstairs, above the pub but the kids will hae tae sleep on the flair. We can arrange a more permanent solution the morrow,' suggested Jock.

The children drew close to their mother at this suggestion. While Rupert instinctively placed his arm round his son. But it was not long before their bedtimes and with no other suggestion available, the family somewhat reluctantly made their way upstairs to investigate the room. It was sparsely furnished but Jock switched on a convector heater to dry their clothes. He brought out several blankets and asked them to make the best they could for the time being. Rupert dreamed of making a claim against the House proprietor; Victoria dreamed of returning to her friends in Surrey for a sleep over to tell her all about her disastrous holiday; Edward was wondering about making a video game which destroyed a house drowning the occupants but Susanna was too tired to dream after her day's exertions. As the midnight hour struck, she removed Rupert's wandering hand. It was an inappropriate night to indulge.

Six hours later the call for breakfast was announced and with sleep in their eyes the Parker-Smythe's emerged from their eyrie into the empty bar where Jock had set a table. On that table were four bowls with hot steam rising from each, a jug of milk and a sugar bowl, salt and pepper were already in position.

'I've never seen this before!' said Rupert.

'Eugh...what's this Mummy?' asked Victoria.

'I'm not eating this!' declared Edward.

'It's good healthy porridge. Put some milk on it and add sugar if you want, the English like it that way. Oh and I've some good news fur ye. You'll be staying at Jim's home for the rest of the sentence.'

The family ate their toast and tea but spoons sank into four porridge bowls. Without a word of thanks, the family folded their blankets and then paraded out of the bar and into the comfort of their car. They returned to the damaged house to retrieve as much personal clothing and effects as they would require at Jim's.

Bob had an early start to call at Bengatton Farm. His arrival alerted a much happier Jim who was there to greet him.

'Good mornin' Jim. You've got guests stayin with you.'

'Good morning Bob. Who'll that be then?' asked Jim.

'It's the one and only Parker-Smythe foursome.'

'But I didna hae the food or money tae keep a' they

hungry mouths. Ye ken that Bob. An anyway, why are they comin? Are they no happy where they are?'

'Jim, let me pit it this way. Tam paid an unofficial visit as it were and accidentally forced the header tank through the ceiling, then the bedroom and finally into the lounge. The house is a disaster zone, believe you me.'

A broad smile came over Jim's face.

'Ah weel Bob, it micht be better if they stay here onyway. They'll be closer tae the sheep. An' I'll get mair work oot o' them. No just 9 to 5 as Dolly Parton sings.'

'Let's see how they manage a straight eight hour day first. Tam will take care o' the food.'

'So when can I expect them?'

'Jim, I'd say any minute now.'

'Oh hell, the place needs a tidy up. The bedrooms are nae ready.'

'Dinny fash yersel Jim. Susanna and the kids wull hae a' day tae make it spic and span.'

Tam appeared with six rabbits over his shoulder heading into the yard. He saw the Range Rover approach. A welcoming committee formed naturally in the courtyard as Rupert drove in.

'Stop the car Daddy,' ordered Victoria.

She wound down her window. She saw the dead rabbits. She spat at Tam who did not flinch.

'You murdering bastard,' she shouts.

Slowly Tam lifted his arm and wiped away the spit from his face. The car pulled up by Jim's front door. Jim who was holding his stick for support, waved them to enter his home.

'Yer welcome. Come on in. I'll show yuz around.'

Jim limped from room to room taking his time to get upstairs with the family following.

'This is the bigger of the two rooms.'

Jim continued to a third room.

'This is Victoria's room, the box room.'

Edward was excited. He would not be sharing a room with his sister after all but where might his room be he wondered.

'And which is my room?' asked Edward.

Jim turned round and placed his hand on Edward's shoulder.

'Edward you have a special treat. You will stay outside in a bothy, with Tam.'

A loud wail came from Edward. He fought through sobs to say:

'Why do I...sob, sob....have to...sob sob...stay outside....sob..with the loser?'

'Edward, right now you think you drew the short straw. But let me tell you, if you watch what Tam does, I promise you will learn some things very useful. Some thin's you might only see aince in a lifetime,'

Edward controlled his sobbing.

'What will that be?' he asked.

'Don't bite the haund that feeds ye.'

'What does that mean?'

'Just take ma word for it sonny. Come on noo, come wi me.'

Jim left the rest of the family to settle into their new quarters. Edward followed Jim downstairs in a ram-stam manner and picked up his rucksack with an aggressive snatch and followed Jim to the bothy.

On Jim's return to the house, he headed for the kitchen to see what he had by way of food for his guests. As he walked he accidentally dropped his stick. When he bent down to retrieve it, he saw for the first time two skinned rabbits. Jim picked them up and placed them in the sink where he found two more skinned rabbits. Bob entered the room as Jim turned round and saw he had yet another couple of skinned rabbits. He added them to the others in the sink.

Jim found a stool and made a comfortable position for him to start cleaning the rabbits when Tam returned with a Tesco bag of mixed vegetables. Jim gave Tam the thumbs up sign. There would be a feast this evening.

Assembling for their second day's work Rupert was last to leave the comfort of Jim's home.

'Come on Rupert. It's time tae round up they sheep.'

'Well actually I've not settled in yet. I've still a few things to unpack,' said Rupert.

'There's plenty o' time fur that whin its dark,' reminded Bob.

'Not those bloody stupid sheep again'.

'Well Rupert, ye did knock ower some folk on the road remember. A Glasca guy wid had got the jail had he done whit you did.'

They continued to walk up the field. Rupert's panting became increasingly audible.

'How many sheep are there Bob?'

'Oh I'd hae tae ask Jim tae git the exact number but at least one thousand five hundred and fifty or so.'

Rupert stops to take in the number.

'And how many acres have you got for that number of sheep?'

'10.'

'That's not a lot', said Rupert indignantly.

'Ten square miles, to be exact.'

'Well that's really a lot of acres.'

'6480 to be precise. Come on let's keep goan. There

could be sheep in difficulty lambing and a' we're doin' is bletherin'.'

Bob set the pace despite his advancing years and soon they came across a ewe in distress. She was exhausted trying to give birth to the lamb. Bob gave instructions.

'Come round, all o' ye. Surround her. Keep the sheep from fleein'. Slowly now....'

The sheep got up and was anxious. It scarpered through the makeshift cordon. The family fell over. But Bob extended his crook and caught the ewe. He grounded her.

'Ye see how quick ye hiv tae be? Noo, which wan o' ye wants tae lamb this ewe?'

As the alpha male in the Parker-Smythe family pack, Rupert offered to be the first midwife! He looked under the sheep's tail to see an emerging head.

'I've found its head. So what do I do now? Pull it out?'

'No. Push its head back in Rupert and find its front legs. Dinnae roose her. Keep her calm.'

'I can't get her head back in, now that it's out!'

'Just wait till it stops pushin'.'

Rupert eventually managed to return the head and tried to feel for the lamb's front legs. Victoria and Suzzane looked on anxiously and Edward sat down in the grass and made a daisy chain with the gowans.

'It's so tight in there, there's no room tae move.'

'Use just one finger. Try tae hook it under its knees and pull forward.'

'Yes...yes...I think it's coming. Yes, I've definitely got them. It's coming.'

'Gently Rupert, easy does it. Wait till she's pushin'. Only when she's pushin' now.'

Then suddenly the lamb is born. Rupert is amazed at the sonsie wee cretur an' sports the broadest of smiles.

'I've done it. Given birth to a lamb! Wonderful! What an experience! Can I do another?'

Not yet mid-wife Rupert. Come an' gie the lamb tae its mother. Let the ewe lick it. An' before ye give yersel anaither pat oan the back, pit yet hand in again. Make sure there's nae mair from where it came fae.'

'No, it just feels like a can of worms.'

'Fine, a good job done,' said Bob.

The family patted Rupert on his back.

'Step awa noo folks. She's ben thru a hard time. Gie her space. Let the ewe take tae its lamb.'

The group move away quietly and continue to the top of the hill. They stop and take in the magnificent view.

'See there Victoria, that dot in the sky? That's whit we ca' the laverock, the skylark.'

'And what do you call the other birds?

'Well the mavis is the thrush and we ca' the blackbird the merle. The lapwing's the pliver and am canty an carlin.'

'And what is canty and carlin?' asked Edward.

'It means I'm cheerful an I'm an old man.'

'You're a wise old man if I may say', added Suzzane.

'But why do you speak that way and use words I've never heard?' asked Edward.

'Well Edward, it's the way my parents spoke an' their parents before them. It's the way we speak to each other here in the south west. We use some words you only hear in Scotland. Now, if I stayed at your home in Surrey, I'd find your friends spoke a strange way too. But for you, that's normal. And that's why yer learnin' how we talk in these parts.'

'Yes, it has been an eye opener indeed,' said Suzzane.

'A breath taking view,' said Rupert.

'Is that Jim's house in the distance? asked Suzzane?

'Aye it is and its downhill a' the way. I guess you'll be ready fur yer lunch.'

'Rather,' said Rupert.

'Then let's go,' said Bob.

At Jim's house there is a warm smell of a cooked dinner to greet them. Inside, the table is set for seven people. Jim served into the bowls and Bob set them on the table.

'Lunchtime folks. Wash yer haunds thoroughly now, then come tae the table,' ordered Bob.

Tired and hungry, the family entered the kitchen but smiled at the pleasant smell of a oven bearing lunch.

'Mmmm this smells good,' said Victoria.

Bob approached wearing oven gloves to protect him from the hot tattie pot. He placed it in the middle of the table. When he took the lid off, they could see butter had melted over it and chives in small flakes had been sprinkled over the tatties like confetti.

'Help yersels. You'll be hungry,' said Jim.

'What is it?' asked Victoria.

'Casserole,' replied Jim.

'Oh great. I am starving,' said Edward.

Jim took out of his Raeburn cooker, a piping hot large casserole dish and placed it on the table besides the tatties. As the serving spoons were placed in the tatties and casserole respectively, Tam entered. He placed his rifle against the wall and took up his place at the table. Suzzane began to serve her family but Jim had his eyes closed and his hands clasped.

'Some hae meat and cannot eat

Some cannot eat that want it;
But we hae meat and we can eat,
Sae let the Lord be thankit. Amen.'

Jim opens his eyes and looks up. Suzzane remains poised with the serving spoon in mid air.

'Let's get stuck in,' said Jim.

Plates were piled high with tatties and casserole, decorated with chopped carrot, peas and turnip finely diced. They all lifted up their cutlery and started to enjoy Jim's fine cooking.

'I don't know whether it's the country air or all the exercise but it's made me hungry and this is the best chicken I've tasted in a long time. My hats off to the chef,' said Rupert.

All are in agreement. Jim glanced at Bob. Bob took a mouthful and looked at him. Jim kicked Bob under the table. Tam at the end of the table shook his head and placed his finger on his closed lips. Jim, in danger of letting out a loud gaffaw, deliberately dropped his knife on the floor. Bob and Jim bend down under the table to pick it up and their heads meet.

'It's rabbit, no chicken,' whispered Bob.

'I know, but they don't know it yet!' said Jim.

They resumed their seated positions and saw how much the meal was going down a treat.

A car is heard to arrive and Jim stands up. With a canty smile he went to the door to greet Jo.

'Come away in dear. Have ye had yer dinner lass?'

'No, not yet. I'm starving though. I've been busy all morning,' said Jo.

'Then make way for the slip o'a lass. There, sit down and take a plate. Help yersel to some tatties and casserole,' invited Bob.

'I certainly will.'

'One of the best chicken casseroles I've ever had Jo. You are in for a treat,' said Rupert.

Jo took a sip of water then lifted her fork and knife. She cut a tattie and covered it with sauce. She balanced it on her fork and smiled.

'Mmmm I had no idea you were such a chef, Jim'

'Hear hear,' said Rupert.

Jo then took some meat from the bone and placed it in her palate.

'Yes a super casserole. It's not chicken though, no,.....it's definitely rabbit,' she said.

The family screw up their faces.

'Euch..Rabbit!' announced Edward.

'It tasted good when you thought it was chicken. Just because it was once a furry bunny doesn't mean we can't enjoy it!' said Jim

'Anyway, its time tae git back tae work.

'But we have hardly just finished our dinner!' protested Rupert.

'The trouble is Rupert, the sheep don't stop for dinner. They lamb at onytime,' said Bob.

'Well I'm not ready, I'm going to the toilet,' said Victoria.

On hearing Victoria's words, Tam banged his fist on the table to attract attention. Victoria looked at him and frowned. When all eyes were upon him, Tam placed his fingers in his throat and feigned a wrenching noise.

'Whatever do you mean?' asked Victoria.

'I think he is trying to tell you Victoria is goan ta make herself sick doon the toilet,' suggested Jim.

'No I am not!' said Victoria.

'If ye don't eat, ye don't shit, you die!' said Jim without decorum.

Suzzane looked disgustedly at Jim briefly; then continued to escort her daughter to the toilet, against her daughter's protestations.

The family are off once again on the hill. Jo cleaned up the lunchtime dishes then asked Jim to sit down so that she could change his dressings. Before she attended to Jim, she checked Jess to find her with a raised temperature. She gave the dog a penicillin pill. She closed her mouth to force the dog to swallow it. The dog having been seen to, Jo now gave her undivided attention to Jim.

'Do you still keep in touch with your wife Jim?'

'Naw, not fur a while noo. Where she is she canna contact me.'

'There's a Ceilidh on Saturday night. Would you like to go?'

'Och, I'd like tae but I've had a big day preparing the meal and the strain o it a'.'

Jo pats his knee. She understood his reluctance but did not see it as a sleight on her. As she rose, she kissed him on the head. Jim smiled. He was a contented man.

The family continued to find ewes with some needing their collective attention.

'I can only dae this till 3pm. I've got ma coos tae milk', said Bob.

Bob hands each family member a whistle with a string to hang round their necks.

'What are these for?' asked Rupert.

'If the mist comes doon suddenly, ye gie them a blaw. That keeps us a' thi gither.'

'But how would we get back in such conditions?' asked Rupert.

'Yer Guardian Angel is lookin' o'er ye all.'

'And who might that be?' asked Rupert.

'Oh that's big Tam.'

'But I can't see Tam,' said Suzanne.

'Look, there he is. Over there!'

'Where?' asked Rupert.

'O'er there, past thae rocks.'

'I still cannot see him,' said Rupert.

Bob blew his whistle and Tam stood up in the distance.

'You know how to lamb now, so if ye need ony further advice, then just blow that whistle. I'll be off noo.'

Jim was looking in the cupboards for an evening meal when the family returned. They flopped into the nearest chairs.

'I can't take much more of this. My legs are sore from all this walking,' said Victoria.

'So are mine,' said Edward.

'You've hardly started yet. Thurs even anaither three hoors tae go the day,' said Jim.

Rupert let out a long tired sigh.

'I wish I had never knocked you down, Jim,' he said.

'So dae a. An' we widnae hud a' this trouble trainin' ye tae be shepherds. It takes years tae get used tae it,' said Jim.

Rupert sat back reflectively.

'Remember in the bar Jim, you said 'you can't eat money'. What did you mean?'

'Well, I havnae got much money but I'm still feedin' ye off the land. That's whur the food comes fae.'

'Oh I see what you meant. If I have all the money but no food, then I have nothing.'

At this time of day after a day's work in the city, Rupert would have his slippers on at home waiting to be called for the evening meal while nursing a whisky. As that thought passed his mind Tam arrived. He stood at the door and motioned as if he was a fish swimming.

'Are you goan fishin' Tam?'

Tam's eyes lit up. He nodded positively.

'Edward, would ye like tae go fishin'? asked Jim.

'Yes. Much better than trekking all over the fields.'

'Ok then follow Tam. Off you go fishin' and don't come back if yer haunds are empty,' Jim laughed.

Tam led Edward to a small burn a little under a mile from Jim's home. Once at the stream, Tam motioned Edward to follow behind as Tam searched for a deep pool.

'Where's your rod Tam. You can't catch a fish without a rod or a hook?'

Tam smiled at Edward. He pointed a finger to his head to show he knew what he was doing. First of all, he knelt by the moving stream and cooled his hands down. Then he opened a plastic bag for Edward to hold. They returned to the deep pool and Tam began to guddle out a small trout. He showed it to Edward and put it back in the stream. He motioned to Edward with both hands to show it was too small. He returned the fish to the pool. Lying flat on the bank, Tam entered his hands once more. A fish showed interest. Tam gently tickled its side then with a deft movement seized the fish. This time he brought out a sizeable trout, then another and another. After Edward had five trout in the bag, Tam stood up and pointed to the farmhouse. Edward is pleased to be given the fish to take back. His family would be impressed.

Edward is first to return. Jim and Rupert are engaged in chatter when he arrived.

'Dad you should have seen how Tam fishes. It's amazing.'

'What do you mean son?'

'Well he puts his cold hands in the water, strokes the fish and flicks them out. He then bangs them on the head to kill them and I've brought them home.'

'You must be joking, Edward. I bet you got them from someone's fridge.'

'No dad, I saw him doing it!'

Rupert looked up to see Tam nodding to confirm his method of fishing. Tam then looked at Jim and saw his smile and nod too. They must have been right. No rod, no net fishing, Tam style fishing he thought.

That evening they sat down to fresh grilled trout with mashed creamed potatoes and boiled carrots. It was a meal which the family relished and no more so than Edward, who recalled once more Tam's unique fishing guddling skills to his sister.

As night fell, all sat satisfied in Jim's lounge. Around a glowing log fire.

'So how long have you been here, Jim? asked Rupert.

'All my life. I was actually born upstairs in the room you have to sleep in.'

'And all the McKenzies at Bengatton farm?'

'About one hundred and twenty five years or so.'

'That's a long time.'

'Aye, it is. But I dinnae ken how much longer I'll be here.'

'Why's that, Jim?' asked Suzanne.

'Well I've come through two foot and mouth

outbreaks last year and the last one hit us hard. Lambs were half the price they were the year before because there were no exports and Britain does nae eat lamb, so we couldnae sell ony lambs fur profit.'

Jim looked up to see the family were interested in what he was saying.

'So now I owe the bank a lot o' money. I don't know how I'm gaun tae pay it back if a don't get a lot o lambs this Spring, so I'm relyin' on you tae take care o' ma flock.'

CHAPTER SEVEN.

CROSSED WIRES

Bob came from his farm to find Jim already in his courtyard. He got out of his old Land Rover and greeted him.

'I've pit thae heifers in Friday's sale at Castle Douglas fur ye. I'll come an' give ye a haund on the morn o' the sale,' said Bob.

'That's great, Bob.'

'Before a' forget like, I've brought some milk fur ye.'

'Brilliant, I wis gettin' low.'

Back in the kitchen, Jim goes straight to his pot on the stove. He gave the porridge a good stir.

'Breakfast ready, Croudie-time again!' he shouted.

A thunder of feet came down to the kitchen. Bowls were already in place and Jim poured milk on his porridge. He is first to start eating, the others are quick to follow on.

'Hmmm...it's a bit salty for me,' said Rupert.

'Aye, that's how we take it traditionally in Scotland. Pour more milk on, it might help,' suggested Jim.

Edward poured more milk into his bowl and then filled his cup with the cold milk.

'Is it from Tesco or Sainsbury's? It's very creamy,' asked Edward.

'That's a secret ma man.'

'So where does it come from?

'It came frae the coo this mornin'.'

Victoria made a large eyed expression then poured the milk into her bowl and cup too.

Once more the family are patrolling the field after breakfast. Rupert and the children are in the lead and first to break the horizon. They find a dead sheep. Edward runs back down the hill, excited to tell Jim about his find.

'Aye son, where ye hiv live stock, ye hiv deed stock too. It's the way o the world.'

'But what can we do with it?' asked Edward.

'Ah telt ye. If it's deed, it's deed. Ye pit it tae one side and carry on tae look after the livin' ones. The survival o' the fittest. That's what it is.'

Edward headed back to his father and sister, with his head hung low. He approached the carcass.

'We have to carry on with the living ones, Jim said.'

The family spread out looking for any other distressed or dead sheep. No other ewes are found. The clouds are much heavier now and the rain began to fall.

'Which way do we go now,'? asked Suzanne.

'I thought you knew,' accused Rupert.

'No I've been following you!'

'We must stay together and if necessary, blow our whistles.'

The family found a large boulder and sat on it. They each held their whistles and blew them in unison but after fifteen minutes, there had been no response.

'It's no use, let's start walking,' said Rupert.

'But which way?' asked Suzanne.

Victoria began to cry.

'We're lost,' she said.

'We must remember to wait for Tam. He'll find us. Remember what Bob said,' said Edward.

Rupert, determined to get off the misty hill, started to walk away from the family. As he disappeared into the mist, a figure appeared from the other side. Tam arrived but Rupert does not see him. Suzzane whistled to her husband as Tam came up to her and placed his hand on her shoulder. The children are pleased and relieved to see Tam but when Rupert returned he was far from happy.

'Where the hell have you been? We've been lost in this downpour whistling for ages. What took you so long?' he demanded.

'Rupert! Come on dear. Don't be like that. Tam's here now, that's what matters.'

With out a word being said, the group are led off the hill and back to Jim's home. Half an hour later lunch is ready.

'Dinner is ready. You'll be hungry after a morning on the hill. How's the lambing goan?' asked Jim.

'Bloody lambing! We were lost most of the time, found one dead sheep, then the rain came down and we sat blowing our whistles till the Cyclops came,' said Rupert.

Jim ignored Rupert's outburst and produced a full plate of salad, ham and mashed potato before him.

'Awe, it's a funny thing the mist, yiv got a respect it though. But it's good tae get back home out o' it too.'

Jim looked out of the window. Jo's car had driven up. Jo slammed the door shut and ran into Jim's house. She was soaked wet from head to tail.

'The taps fell off the sink at the back of the surgery; there's water running out the door. I need help.'

'You need a plumber. Noo, where's the Yellow pages?' asked Jim.

'I need to find the stop cock,' said Jo.

As Jim started to search for the directory, Tam appeared.

'Looks like yiv gotta plumber already!'

Rupert cleaned his plate and piped up from the sink.

'I'll help as well.'

'No Rupert. You're still on the lambing,' said Jim.

'We can't do lambing in this fog!'

'Then let's all go down to the surgery tae help.'

In Jo's car and Rupert's, they all went to the surgery.

Tam found the water cock under a log at the side of the surgery but it did not respond to his turning. There was no time to overcome this difficulty. Jim looked into the wasteland behind the surgery. The grass had never been cut and was waist high.

'Tam, you'll hae tae dae yer stuff.'

'What stuff? asked Rupert.

'Jist watch him!'

Tam took out a knife and took a piece of wire from the garden fence. He cut them in two pieces about a foot and a half long then bent each piece at an angle of ninety degrees.

'What the hell's he up to, the water is still leaking for goodness sake!' said Rupert.

'Jist watch him, I telt ye.'

Tam held the wires in front of him and started to walk slowly across the garden. Almost halfway across, the wires met very quickly. Tam turned towards the onlookers and walked up to within two yards of the window. Tam started to dig with the heel of his boot, to the amazement of Rupert. He uncovered a metal plate with the word 'water' written on it. He knelt down, opened the metal plate and put his hand in to turn off the water.

'Quite amazing. Did you see that children? How does he do that?' asked Rupert.

Tam approached Rupert and placed two wires in his hands. Rupert walked forward but nothing happened. Tam walked up to Rupert, he pulled him back a bit, he then placed one finger on his wrist and the wires rotated. Rupert drops the wires as if they were live!

'That's not right. That's weird. What's this mumbo jumbo?'

'No not mumbo jumbo as you say Rupert. It's what some call water dousing,' clarified Jim.

Jim limped back to the surgery to help Jo clear up. She is so pleased that the water has stopped that she gave Jim a hug and a cuddle then a kiss. Jim smiled and gave her a peck on the cheek but is aware that the family are around, he gets flustered and blushed.

'I'll hiv tae get back tae work, dear.'

Jim walked back to the car with a satisfied smile on his face. Rupert saw the smile.

'Yes, quite remarkable how Tam stopped the water.'

'Aye', smiled Jim, 'quite remarkable! Now time to get round the ewes for the last time today.'

A groan is heard from the children. A bass groan came from Rupert.

CHAPTER EIGHT

BROWN COW IN THE RING

The following day was market day. The cattle were led out on to the loading bank and then they entered their pens. Rupert parked and brought his family through a crowd of people from near and far and entered the ring.

'Have a seat. Oor cattle are no in for a wee while. But don't make any unnecessary movements.'

'Why Jim?' asked Rupert.

'Cos I don't want tae go hame wi mair cattle than a came wi, that's why!'

'How do you mean?'

'Well, scratch yer heid, rub yir chin, nod yir head or have eye contact wi' the auctioneer and your bids in.'

'Oh I see. I've got you now. Did you understand that children?'

More cows are sold with the auctioneer in full swing speaking like a runaway train in a language all of his own but known to all the farmers. Then Jim's heifers come in. Jim moved up to the auctioneer's stand. The auctioneer nodded at him and the sale was underway.

'In-calf heifers fae Bengatton,' called the auctioneer.

The sale started at £500 and the bidding increased to £600. All the cattle are sold. Jim shook the auctioneer's hand and left. He returned to sit with Rupert and his family.

'Well did you enjoy that?'

'Yes, it was quite exciting', said Victoria

'Well how did the sale go?' asked Rupert.

'It wisnae bad. It could hiv been worse.'

'Was it a good price then?'

''Rupert, I've probably made aboot £50 -£60 a head o cattle.'

'Is that all?'

'Aye, that's the margin I made the day. It wis nay too buoyant.'

Rupert gasped then boasted.

'I wouldn't get out of my bed in the morning to make that sort of money.'

'It's no aboot makin' money. Hae a good look at a' the faces aroon' the ring.'

'I guess all a bit on the old side.'

'Aye an' who'll be here in ten years time tae get the food oan the table?'

Jim looked into Rupert's eyes with a cold stare. Bob stood behind the pair feeling the friction.

'That's why we call Jim, the Last Shepherd.'

Rupert reflected on what Bob had said.

'Do you mean we could all starve in ten years?'

'Might be before ten years are up. The food is startin' tae come fae abroad the noo.'

'What can we do about that then,' asked Edward.

'It's not up tae you or us. It's got tae come fae the government but they are like the three wise monkeys!' said Jim.

Jim put his hand in his pocket. He brought out some crunched up notes and started to walk round the ring. He tapped one man on the shoulder and gave him some money. He does this to four other men then limped back towards Rupert with his head held high and out of the cattle market he strode. Rupert and his family followed on bewildered.

Rupert ran after Jim. He asked him what he was doing dishing out money to the men.

'I was given' them a lucky penny.'

'What do you mean, a lucky penny?'

Jim stopped turned round and in front of Rupert and his family explained what he had done.

'Well Rupert, it's like this. You could take a heifer home from the market but it could lose a calf. Become unwell, it might even die. There's no come back, no damaged goods agreement. So that's why we give a lucky penny.'

Back at Bengatton farm, Bob helped Jim from the car.

'Well Rupert, time tae get back up the field an' look fur the sheep.'

To Jim's surprise, Rupert is enthusiastic having spent the morning at the market. He is eager to return to the fields.

'OK Family, let's get up there. Come on, let's go.'

Jim and Bob had arched eyebrows seeing the family's sudden enthusiasm for farming. They joined in at a much more leisurely pace. Jim whispered to Bob.

'Over there! Look, o'er the dyke. Look.'

'I see it. Thirs a braw set o' antlers oan it. Whirs Tam when ye need him?'

'What d'ya mean? asked Jim

Bob chuckled.

'Yer menu's no had venison yet!'

'So?'

They watch the deer on the horizon. The deer moved slightly towards their direction for a moment then the deer fell to the ground. It rolled on its back. Then an arm appeared briefly. The hand contained a knife and in a swift action, the knife entered the deer's neck. A short struggle ensued. Tam stood up and with the deer bent over his shoulders, he made his way down off the hill.

'Bloody hell. Ye don't see that every day. Quick, incisive, brutal but professional.'

'You're right Jim. But I've heard he's done that before. It gives a new meaning to deer stalking.'

They catch up on Rupert and his family.

'What's wrong?'

'Nothin,' said Jim.

Rupert searched the skyline but saw nothing.

'Well I can't see anything. What were you looking at?'

'You could look a' day Rupert, but yid niver see it.'

Rupert shook his head. All these tricks played on his mind. Why could he not see what they were seeing? Was an inner sight given to those who worked the land? Well maybe there was, and a townie like him would never see like them, and that feeling frustrated him but also gave him some contentment. This was only a holiday after all. Well perhaps not a holiday in the true sense of the meaning. A sentence? No that would be a little too harsh. An educational experience seemed a more apt description of what he was experiencing.

CHAPTER NINE

UNDERNEATH THE BONNET

Jock was busy working at his garage. A car arrived in the village and pulled up beside the pub. Sergeant Billy Cooper and Corporal Gary Flynn both of the SAS (Special Air Services) walked over to Jock while some boys were playing street football. The ball struck the visitor's car and rolled into the garage. Jock picked the ball up and remonstrated with the boys.

'How many times hiv I telt ye? Dinnae play footba' on the street. Go tae the field o'er there. That's where ye can play.'

The two strangers stood on either side of Jock as he held the football under his arm.

'Are you Jock?' asked Sergeant Billy Cooper.

'An' who wants tae know?' replied Jock defensively.

'It's about your friend Tom', said Corporal Gary Flynn.

'I dinnae ken onyone ca'd Tom.'

'He was killed in Afghanistan almost three weeks ago,' said Sergeant Cooper.

'Ye mean big Tam?

'Aye that's what he was known as.'

'Here, ye'd better come inside.'

Jock opened the door from the garage into the pub. Before he showed the visitors in, he took the football to one of the boys, bent down and whispered in his ear. He then pretended to playfully kick the lad's bum and then he kicked the ball back to the boys. The boys scatter going different ways. But the boy who got the earful from Jock cycled down to a gate where he put his hand on a post and opened an orange sign. At this field sign he opened and closed it repeatedly. Jock nodded his approval then entered the pub to speak to his army guests.

'Would ye like a drink or a cuppa?'

'Coffee's fine for me', said Sergeant Cooper.

'Come through tae the kitchen an' hae a seat.'

They sat down with their backs to the back door. Jock boiled a kettle and prepared the mugs.

'So who are yous two?

'I'm sergeant Billy Cooper and this is Coporal Gary Flynn.'

'Sugar?'

'Yes two sugars for both of us and milk to if you can spare it.'

'Och I can aways spare some milk in the country. So which regiment?'

'We're based at Hereford.'

The kettle boiled. Jock filled the mugs and brought them over with a shaky hand.

'So tell me whits this a' aboot?'

'We were on the Afghan/Pakistan border acting as observers on Taliban movements when a convoy of Humbies pulled up right below.'

Jock raised his eyes with interest to hear their story.

'That was when the Americans got out and started to walk towards a group of hidden Taliban fighters on a nearby ridge. Then they realised the man in front was wearing the British uniform of the Royal Engineers.'

Jock was listening intently while stirring his mug of coffee as he did so.

'Well this man's face was covered with blood and his eyes were swollen. His hands were tied with cable ties. We got straight on to the satellite phone and through to HQ and asked if any British personnel were missing. I was put on hold but we could not wait for a reply.'

Simultaneously they drank from their mugs. The boys playing football in the field behind occasionally let a shout penetrate the tense atmosphere.

'We didn't have time on our side. The Taliban were about to strike. I was looking through the scope on my rifle and described the man to Sergeant Cooper.'

'That's right. He reported the man was big, holding something dangling from his hands.'

'The man fell over and the trooper behind him was shot dead by a Taliban sniper. The rest of the Americans took cover except for one. The British soldier got back to his feet and then the American soldier shot him in the back with his hand gun, much to our horror.'

'I started to shout down the phone asking for fresh orders,' said Sergeant Cooper.

'The big man was still moving. What happened next was unbelievable.'

Jock sipped his coffee and offered some Glengarrie

biscuits around. As Sergeant Cooper crunched his biscuit, he continued the tale of horror.

'Tam, as you call him, got the knife from the dead trooper and cut himself free. He got up and went for the Americans head on, armed only with a knife. He got so close that he could not be shot at. He started hand to hand combat killing them one by one, stabbing and lashing out at them under their body armour, lifting some men off the ground as he thrust forward. Then we gave up on the phones and started to shoot at the Americans.'

'Thereafter we heard incoming American reinforcements. Tam disappeared behind a Humbie. The firing stopped. Then I saw around ten Americans pushing Tam to the ground. They lay on top of him, his heads only being exposed. One came up to him and shot him in the head. Point blank range.

'Good God,' said Jock.

'We lost it. I can tell you. We gave them everything we had until we heard air support approaching. I got on to the phones and heard them say that they had lasers on Taliban positions. We also had lasers and painted them with it. Then they dropped the bombs. We waited. The bombs fell on the American troops.'

'That was when we heard a cheer from the Taliban positions. We were sickened by what had taken place. We are sorry to bring this sad news to you about your friend. He was a very brave man. '

'We would have liked to have known him. He was so very special,' added Sergeant Cooper.

A masked eye looked through the window. Jock noticed it and shook his head to indicate don't come in but Tam did not see the signal, the handle of the door turned.

'We feel bad because we could not save your friend,' said Corporal Flynn.

Jock gave a parental smile.

'That's all right boys. You can meet him now. He's standin' richt behind you!'

The two soldiers stand up and turn round.

'Jesus Christ!' said Sergeant Cooper

'You're still alive Tam?' asked Corporal Flynn redundantly.

Tam nodded. He put away his blood stained knife from his clenched fist in his leg pocket.

'Do you two want tae spend the nicht here? Seems you have a lot to say to each other. Mind Tam canna speak but he can listen and let you ken what he's thinkin'.

'Yes sir, That'll be magic. And we understand it won't be easy.

The two soldiers walked across the bar floor to the front door to gather their luggage. They opened the door. They are met by a crowd of around fifteen men armed with pitch forks, brushes, guns and a rifle. Jock barged through the soldiers to speak to them.

'No, they're friendlies. They are on oor side as it were. I'll be able tae tell ye more later, but there's nothin' tae git vexed aboot.'

'What the hell was that all about?' asked Sergeant Cooper.

'Well, it's like this. Back in Afghanistan Tam was drillin' wells for the local folk. One mornin' a small girl disappeared. She coudnae be foond onywhir. That was when Tam asked her mother for some claes or a blanket o' the girls so that he could fin' her. Tam was eventually given a blanket by a bemused mother. He then took a necklace from roond his neck an' held it up. It hung swingin' awa fae him. So he followed the line o' the necklace tae an auld well where they foond the girl at the very bottom o' it. Fortunately she wisnae badly injured an' the villagers were amazed and delighted at the way in which Tam, hid foond the lassie. That wis when the named him the Angel.'

'What a lovely story' said Corporal Flynn.

'Aye bit some Americans in the village heard o' the rescue technique an' were mighty interested. So they asked if they could use his skills tae find Usama bin Laden. When Tam told him he wouldn't, because he couldn't, the Americans took him away and tortured him to persuade him to cooperate and find Usama bin Laden.'

They gathered their luggage and were shown to their room upstairs, previously vacated by the Parker-Smythes.

'Noo, the only reason Tam refused tae find Usama bin Laden was that if he was caught, his home village would be blown to pieces. That means here in oor wee pairt o' the world. So when they saw you two comin' they thought you were Americans to blow up oor village!'

'I'm glad to be on your side' said Sergeant Cooper.

In the evening Rupert and the family sat at the table. Jim served a plate of tatties. He then served some venison burgers. The family ate them with relish, and with real relish! They hardly noticed Jo arrive. She looked quite stunning. She was out of her work clothes and had washed her hair. Her tight fitting sweater brought her figure to notice.

'Jim, well are you going to the Ceilidh at the village hall?'

'Aye, but it looks like I'll need tae brush up a wee bittie.'

'Can anyone go? Is it open to all?' asked Rupert.

'Aye, of course, we can all go down.'

Tam shook his head. He looked at the table.

'Who wants the last tattie?' asks Jim.

Rupert with fork in hand goes to spear the tattie. He lifted his arm and thrust it down onto the plate at the same time Tam picked up the last tattie with his hand. Rupert's fork stuck into the back of Tam's hand. Tam carried on as if nothing happened.

'Tam! Do you not feel the fork in your hand?' asked Jo.

Tam looked at Jo then his hand. Rupert had a worried look on his face and is not sure whether to sit, run, or retrieve the fork. He looked at Jo then Jim for some support. Tam pulled the fork from the back of his hand and wiped his blood on his sleeve. He then cut the potato in half, speared the half tattie with his blood stained fork and handed it back to Rupert.

'I am sorry,' said Rupert nervously.

'You'd better eat it, or he'll be offended,' suggested Jim.

Rupert looked at his wife and children and slowly placed the fork in his mouth. He chewed the tattie with a sour expression. The meal finished. The plates were cleared. Jim placed all the dirty dishes in the sink.

'Victoria and I will wash up. Jim, you get ready for the dance,' said Suzzane.

Jim limped upstairs to get ready.

'I am sorry Tam. Are you all right?' said Rupert.

Tam gave Rupert the OK sign with his thumb and forefinger.

A few minutes later Jim arrived down in a dress suit.

Jo's eyes lit up. She smiled and tiptoed up to give him a kiss.

'Jim, are you sure Tam is OK? After all he did not seem to feel that fork in his hand?'

'I don't really know. It's not good is it? Anyway tonight, let's get to the ceiligh.

CHAPTER TEN

A GRAVE MISTAKE

The ceiligh was in full swing. Scottish country music was heard all down the street. The Ceilidh band played at the bar end of the hall. Two fiddlers, a drummer, an accordionist and a clarinettist made the local band. And they were always popular. Twenty six people danced in the body of the hall through the Canadian barn dance, the Gay Gordons, and Strip the Willow, Orcadian style. They got their breath back at the bar. The fast dances Jim could not join in but when the violinist played a slow waltz, Jo led him onto the floor and all eyes realised the Last Shepherd was recuperating well and the young vet was part of his healing process. When the music ended, they reluctantly separated.

'What will you have Jo?'

'I'm still on call. And driving you home later! Don't forget.'

Jim bought a couple of drinks and a girl brought them over on a tray to where Jo was seated. Jim limped over and sat beside her. They tapped their feet to the music. It was almost too loud to speak. But when another slow waltz began, Jo got Jim up and on the floor. As they danced, the door opened and Rupert arrived with his wife and family. Rupert bought a round of drinks and they sat at the table where Jim and Jo had been seated. When the music ended, Jo and Jim returned to their table. The band began to play a Strathspay.

'That's funny music,' Edward said.

'Scottish country dance music, unique to Scotland. Some real culture at last on your final day. Aren't you due to return south tomorrow?'

'I wish I could stay here forever but we've got to get back to the rat race, you know what it's like,' said Rupert.

'You mean to earn some more money?'

'Don't start that up again!'

'Well you will run over these vagrants on the road.'

'No, there was no vagrant, just a hard working shepherd and his faithful dog.'

'Well then don't make it a habit from now on'.

'If we all did, we'd soon get hungry. I've more than learned my lesson Jim. I assure you of that.'

The final dance was called. Everyone stood up. Jo grabbed Rupert and Jim pulled Suzzane with the children on to the floor. Jo made sure the males alternated between the females. Auld Lang Syne was played. The gathering sang lustily. When they got to the third and fourth verses, thoughts of Edward making daisy chains and guddlin' the trout came to mind:

We twa hae run aboot the braes
And pou'd the gowans fine
But we've wandered monie a weary fit
Sin auld lang syne

We twa hae paidl'd in the burn
Frae morning sun till dine
But seas between us braid hae roar'd
Sin auld lang syne.

And after each verse the chorus was sung. With five verses requiring the chorus soon Rupert was bellowing out the chorus in a fine tenor voice, albeit with some anglicised vowels. But at the last verse the hands broke off. They crossed their hands to link up again with their neighbour and the congregation sang even more loudly:

And there's a hand my trusty fiere
And gie's a hand o' thine,
And we tak a right guid-willie-waught
For Auld Lang Syne

For auld lang syne, my jo
For auld lang syne
We'll tak a cup o' kindness yet,
For Auld Lang Syne.

And as the last chorus was sung, the circle of friends moved forward contracting the circle then expanding it in a final shake of the hands.

They all cheered and thanked the Ceilidh band. Suzzane declared that there was nothing quite like it and Rupert was in full agreement. Jim returned to his table to finish off his glass of whisky and Jo took his hand as they left the hall.

'Noo you twa, don't be doin' onythin' I widnae dae myself,' was Bob's sound advice for the night but Jo recognised his advice was slightly tarnished by the drink.

She drove Jim back to his home and led him back to the house.

'Can I get you a coffee before you head back?' asked Jim.

'Now is that real coffee, or a coded message?

'Jist coffeee....I think.

Jim filled the kettle.

'Oh you're a disappointment I was hoping you had some other kind of stimulant.'

Jo placed her hand on his, on the kettle. She removed his hand and turned to face him in a clench. They kissed. They embraced.

'Let's go upstairs, to bed.'

Jim took the kettle off the boil and turned off the kitchen light. Jo led him upstairs.

In the early hours of the next day, with a shaft of light beginning to enter the bedroom, Jim and Jo were fast asleep. Jim half wakened and was aware once more that he was not alone. The whisky has lessened its grip on his mind and instinctively Jim turned and placed his arm around Jo's naked body.

'I love you. I love you so much Mary.'

Jo heard his declaration and it perturbed her. She sat up in bed.

'My name is Jo not Mary', she said indignantly.

She threw back the covers and marched smartly naked to where her clothes lay strewn about the floor recalling the final abandoned happy moments before they fell asleep the previous night. She was dressed in an instant, slipping her shoes on as she left the room. Jim came to at last.

'Where are you going Jo?'

'Oh you've remembered my name now!'

'What do you mean?'

'You called me Mary don't you remember? Thought you were making love to Mary last night. Oh how to turn a girl off a man instantly.'

'Sorry Jo.'

But Jim's apology was not heard. The front door slammed shut and before Jim got out of bed, Jo's car was already heading down the road. He put on his dressing gown, looked out of the bedroom window and shook his head. He looked back at his bed. Heads had dented both pillows for the first time in quite a while and as things stood Jim could not imagine that sight recurring. He had blown it big time and he knew it. He went down to make some porridge. Shortly afterwards, Rupert came down in high spirits.

'Good morning Jim. Did Jo stay here last night?'

'Good morning. Aye she did.'

'I've seen it coming for some time now. I just knew you two would hit it off.'

'How did you mean?'

'Surely you've seen the way she looks at you? She's fancied you for a while. And Jim, take my word, that's something I do know a little about!'

Jim was not amused and gave Rupert a leering look as he stirred the porridge in the pot. Rupert saw that he has caused some tension.

'I'll get dressed now...and start to pack,' he said.

The children arrived and sat at the table. Jim served small bowls of porridge for them.

'I'll not miss this stuff when I'm gone,' said Victoria.

'Nor me. Where's Tam, Jim?'

'He will have been oan the hill since first light. Why?'

'Oh we want to ask him something,' said Edward.

'Your parents can serve themselves, they know it's in the pot.'

Jim left his house and mounted his tractor. The tractor stops at the garage where Jock has already opened up for business. They greet each other.

'It wis a gud night last night. Did you enjoy it Jim?'

'Aye, I did. Hive ye seen Jo the day by ony chance?'

'Aye. She wis here earlier but she left on a call a wee whilie ago.'

'Ok that's fine. I'll just leave the tractor here an' walk doon tae the kirk if that's a'right wi ye?'

'The kirk? Aye, that's fine Jim. That's jist grand. Ony time, aye ony time, jist leave the car here.'

Jim set off walking with his stick. It took him a few minutes to get to the kirk but his thoughts byke in his head. Out of earshot, Jo arrived at the garage from her call.

'Morning Jock. Is that Jim's tractor?'

'Hi Jo. Aye, it is.'

'Is he around?'

'Aye, jist down the side, aff tae the kirk tae see Mary again. He comes tae see her every noo an' then.'

'Does he now. Well I want to meet this Mary too!'

Jock looked confused. But Jo had a determined walk underway and she was not around for him to clarify her thinking.

The mossy path drowned any footsteps and as Jo entered the churchyard she saw Jim's back and he was in conversation. She slowly approached out of sight. With each step his words became clearer.

'Ye see, I've met some wan else. I really like her so, ma visits tae ye will no be so many. It wouldn't seem right, not so, ma dear?'

Jo edged herself around a bush to see who Jim was addressing his remarks to but could only see a wall. Jo walked up to Jim and is surprised to find him alone.

'Hi. Caught you!

'What di yi mean Jo?'

Jo moved closer to see if anyone was hiding. But the name of Mary McKenzie is written in fresh gold leaf on the headstone before her.

'Jim, you did not tell me Mary was dead!'

'I know. I hiv no been able tae let Mary go, till you came intae ma life.'

Jo knelt down beside Jim. She placed her hand on his shoulder.

'What happened Jim?' she asked.

'Mary died in childbirth last year. They both lie in this grave. The gither in the same coffin.'

'Oh Jim, that will take a long time to get over.'

'They say time is a great healer but ye niver forget the memories do you?'

'No, the memories are yours forever Jim, they're yours for all time.'

After a few minutes at the grave, they stood up and Jo walked hand in hand with Jim back to the garage. The clouds were gathering. They quickened their steps.

Eventually they arrived back at the garage as Rupert's car approached.

'Time for the farewells it seemed,' said Jo

But Rupert looked roosed. His head hung out of his window.

'Have you seen Edward and Victoria? We havn't seen them since breakfast. We've no idea where they could be.'

'They'll be oot oan the hill wi Tam.'

'But we saw Tam at a distance and he was definitely alone.'

'Then we'd better hae a good look fur them. They canna be far awa.'

The tractor and the Land Rover set off back to Bengatton. Rupert followed on behind them tooting his horn all the time. The wind got up. The day lost its light with the dark clouds descending. A bitter wind came from the north.

CHAPTER ELEVEN

LOST IN THE SNOW

At the farm Jim saw Suzzane running around the outhouses.

'Suzzane, hiv ye checked Victoria's room. See if anything is missin',' suggested Jim.

'I've done that. Her jacket, boots and mobile are missing. They are always by her bedside.'

'Quick, to Edward's room in the bothy. Have a thorough look there Rupert,' said Jim.

A few moments later Rupert and Suzzane return as anxious as any parent in the situation.

'The same things are missing in Edward's room. No outdoor shoes, no jacket, no mobile,' said Suzzane.

'We've got a problem oan oor haunds. Jo, go and get Bob.

Jo smartly set off in her car and Jim's worried look upset Rupert.

'What's up Jim? What are you thinking?'

'The forecast is no good. Snaw is expected oan the hills an' high winds,' said Jim.

Rupert twiddled the knob on his radio to get a weather forecast. Jim went over to the bothy to check Tam's room. He searched around Tam's dishevelled room.

'Oh shit! His rucksack is missing.' As he swears, the first flickers of snow began to fall.

As Jim returned and is in the middle of the yard, he met Rupert.

'The forecast is not good at all. Blizzards are expected on the hills with wind up to one hundred miles an hour!' said Rupert.

When Jo arrived at Bob's home, she informed him about the developments. Bob said he'd go straight to inform the police. Despite the snow deepening every few minutes, Bob ran as fast as he could to the police station.

'Easy now Bob, runnin' like that will no be good fur ye. Whait's the matter?' asked PC Sandy Dunn.

'It's the kids. Victoria and Edward, jist vanished.'

'The mountain rescue team are already oot on anaither job but I'll radio them to be vigilant. Noo gee me sum mair details. When did they go missin', where were they seen last; whit were they wearin'. Come on sit doon and get yer breath back Bob. I need this information tae pass oan tae the rescue boys.'

After providing all the details he could remember Jo giving him, Bob set out once more to the pub to spread the word. When he got there the two SAS men were inside with Jock.

'Bob, I'm lookin' fur volunteers. We've twa kids missin' up at Jim's an' he needs help.'

The two soldiers stood up and came forward. We've got our army Land Rover,' said Sergeant Cooper.

'I've got a stretcher, fae the Police station if ye can take that?'

'Certainly can,' said Corporal Flynn.

'Let's get up tae Bengatton.'

The wind-screen wipers slapped furiously, but visibility was negligible. The wind buffeted the Land Rover despite its four-wheel drive base. At Bengatton Jim had to restrain Rupert.

'If yi go oot oan they hills, you'll die, Rupert.'

'But what about my children?'

'We'll find them. But you mist stay here. I'll tell you whit a think his happened.'

Jim released Rupert's jacket and they sat down by the table.

'Well, what then?' asks Suzzane.

'Your son an' daughter hiv asked Tam where they can git a good mobile signal. Tam will hae pointed tae the tap o Benmaghrochan Hill because that's the highest point aboot they parts.'

Rupert looked at Suzanne. The theory was plausible.

'I think Tam is awa tae find them the noo, cos his rucksack case is missin'.'

Light had faded fast. The blizzard continued. A lonely figure was only just visible. Victoria was following the light on her mobile phone to see where she is going. When suddenly, a strong arm grabbed her around the waist and lifted her off the ground. Victoria gave an initial frightened yell but she soon realised it was Tam come to rescue her when she shined her light into his masked face. Tam put her down and grabbed her hand firmly. Victoria froze and Tam knew hyperthermia followed.

A gust of wind blew Victoria off her feet but Tam picked her up. Tam then stopped in a slightly sheltered spot and began to dig furiously like a man possessed of the devil. Before long he had made a snow hole large enough for both of them. He placed Victoria in the hole and got in behind her.

'Find Edward!' she shouted.

Tam shook his head. Victoria became tearful and insistent.

'Please find Edward, please. You must find him. He is up here somewhere,' pleaded Victoria.

Tam pulled out the necklace he wore around his neck. It dangled before Victoria's eyes. It bent towards her like a magnet was pulling inside it. Then in a delft move Tam pulled out a doll. Victoria's doll. Victoria grabbed her doll but saw the motion of the necklace stop.

'Ah, I see. You need something of Edwards!'

Tam smiled at her.

'I'm wearing Edward's scarf!'

Victoria took the scarf from her neck and gave it to Tam. She then curled down in the snow hole as Tam went out to search for Edward. Tam struggled in the whiteout conditions searching for any signs of Edward. Tam walked a further fifty yards then he turned back. He fell on his hands and knees and began clawing at the snow. Eventually a hand appeared, then an arm. He dug furiously and uncovered Edward's body. He checked for any vital sign of life on his young body then gathered him over his shoulder and took him towards the snow hole. He stumbled with his load. Tam was exhausted.

He grabbed Edward by the collar and dragged him along using his knife as an aide. In time he returned to the snow hole and dragged Edward inside beside Victoria who was tired and sleepy. Tam shook her. She wakened. He placed Edward close to her.

'You've found Edward. Oh thank you Tam, Thanks a million.'

Tam searched in his rucksack. To his surprise he found only the empty sleeping bag cover. He looked out of the snow hole, the conditions were still impossible to combat. He turned to look at the unconscious body of Edward lying in the hole. And he looked up at Victoria with a saddened expression. He took off his coat. He wrapped it around the children and rubbed Edward until he gained consciousness in the warmth of the coat and the warmth of his sister.

'But what about you Tam? You have nothing to keep you warm.'

Tam responded with the OK sign and lay down across their legs for the night.

At the farmhouse, Rupert and Jim were pacing up and down the kitchen floor. Suzzane sat with her head in her hands and tears streamed from her face. The two SAS men were seated around the warm range.

'When are you going to find Victoria and Edward?

Jim glowered at Rupert.

'This is hard Rupert. But at the moment the weather is too severe. Just listen tae that oot there. You'd be lucky if ye got mair than twenty yards before the wind wid blew ye o'er. It's no a walk in Hyde Park. This is life and death and at the minute Rupert, I'm sorry tae say, we're lookin' at death in the face.'

Rupert did not respond immediately. He thought through what Jim had said.

'I feel the same way. My heart says I want to get out

there to help but my head tells me you're right. If I went I'd never get back.'

'Don't say that,' said Jo.

'No, he's dead right. You can't see anything in a white out. That wind would cut through you like a knife. It's even hard to breath in, save alone climb a hill in search of two kids,' said Sergeant Cooper.

'But don't forget, Tam's up there lookin' fur them. That's thir best chance. If he finds them, he'll try tae get them some shelter an' keep warm till help arrives. We are that help, so we must ride out the storm, then act.'

Jim walked over to a cabinet, opened the door of it and pulled out a rucksack by his feet. He pulled out a heavy jacket and put it on. He turned round and zipped it up. Jo spotted a mountain rescue badge on the lapel.

'You didn't tell me you were with the Mountain Rescue service Jim,' said Jo.

'I don't advertise it, I only need this in an emergency - when someone goes missin'.

Jim took a small red vest from the cabinet and approached Jess in the corner. He put her front leg in one of the harness straps and went to slip the strap under her other front leg but realised it was not there. Jo grabbed Jim by the arm and pulled him round.

'You can't be serious about this Jim. Taking Jess out in that storm! She'll last not more than five minutes. Remember she's hardly been out of the house since the accident, she'll die in the cold with you!'

Jim looked fearful but adamant.

'Don't you think I know that?'

Jo began to cry and sat down at the table. Suzzane came to comfort her, placing her arm round her shoulders. From his fireside position, Sergeant Cooper stood up and spoke.

We'll come with you. We've been on arctic training in the past couple of years and this is what this is.'

'I'll need you two tae carry the stretcher and casualty bag up the hill.'

We have three radios. A satellite phone is in the Land Rover,' said Corporal Flynn.

'Gary, go and fetch them.'

Corporal Gary Flynn went to get the radios from the car. As he went through the front door a blast of snow entered the house. Flynn returned with the radios.

'Good work. I'll take one radio. We'll leave one at the farm house and the other radio we'll need to keep in contact. Right, when the weather breaks, I'm goan tae head up the ridge and Jess and I will start a sweep search of Benmagrochan until I find them and then I'll get on the radio. Corporal you start half an hour later on the hill.'

Corporal Flynn saluted Jim. Jim looked twice at him.

'Sorry sir, just a habit!'

Rupert stood holding Suzzane's shoulders eagerly listening to the unfolding plans.

'Thank you Jim,' he said.

'I'm nut doin' it fur your kids. I'm doin' it fur Tam because your kids will be dead unless Tam has found them'.

Such plain talking hurt Suzzane who cried.

'You're a heartless bastard saying that,' said Rupert.

'I'm sorry. But in cases like this you have live people and dead people. That's a'I'm sayin'.'

Some time had passed. The wind had died down. It was becoming lighter. Rupert and Suzzane had their arms folded on the table supporting their sleeping heads. Jo is asleep in the armchair.

Jim slipped out quietly with Jess in his arms. He was met by the two SAS men and Bob joined them.

'It takes some guts tae go oot in this. I wish I could come wi' ye,' said Bob.

'Sorry Bob. You've got yersel the baby sittin' job.'

Jim walked passed Bob with Jess still in his arms. He headed off into the snow and started his assent on Benmagrochan. He headed along a ridge where the snow was not so deep and placed Jess down. Jim pulled his crook out of his rucksack and started following his trusty Jess. They walked a couple of miles before Jess picked up a scent. Jess was tired and cold. She could only manage a whimper when indicating a possible contact. Jim, thirty yards behind his collie, ran to Jess grabbing at his thigh as he did so. He found a small hole in the snow. Jess laid down, her work done.

Jim attacked the snow hole and very soon found two figures wrapped in Tam's jacket. One had a ski mask on. Jim shook them and called their names.

'Tam, wake up,' he calls.

Jim placed his fingers on Edward's neck to see if he was alive. Jim then does the same to Tam's neck. Jim's eyes open in confusion as he pulled off the ski mask to find Victoria under it.

'Oh Christ!'

Jim moved back and cleared a tear from his eye and a lump from his throat. He then cleared more snow revealing an arm wearing a T shirt. Victoria wakened.

'Where's Tam,' asked Victoria.

'It's all right dear.'

Jim cleared snow from around his head. He placed

Tam's own balaclava on his head. He dragged Tam's body out of the snow hole. Once he was out he noticed Jess lying motionless with staring eyes on her side. He placed his hand on her. She is as cold as the snow. She is dead. Jim fumbled for the radio.

'Jim One, Jim One to Cooper, over'.

'Cooper receiving Jim one over.'

In the farm yard all gather round Sergeant Cooper's radio.

'Two alive; one dead. Need immediate helicopter evacuation. Over.'

'Received and understood. We have your location. Over and out.'

Sergeant Cooper then opened up the satellite phone.

Jim placed a blanket over the sleeping children. Then a crackling sound alerted him to the satellite phone. He left the snow hole to pick up the signal.

'Say again?'

'We've contacted a helicopter out of HMS Gannet. The 'copter is en route from Arran with a pregnant woman on board. They are diverting to rendezvous and pick you up in approximately ten minutes, repeat ten minutes. Over.'

'That's great but too late for some, over and out.'

Jim looked at Jess and Tam lying motionless in the snow.

At the farm house Rupert and Suzzane are agitated beyond belief.

'Who's dead, ask who's dead. We need to know, it's our children for God's sake. Forget all this jargon and get straight to the point. Who is dead and who is alive?

Bob gives Jim a call.

'Jim, we need to know who is dead?'

'Nut any of the one's we thought at first.'

'Tam?'

'Aye Bob, Tam's dead.'

Bob shared the news with Rupert and Suzzane.

He slumped down in a chair drained from a sleepless night and the loss of a unique friend. Susanna and Rupert are ecstatic.

'The kids are alive! Wonderful,' shouted Rupert.

'Thank God,' declared Suzzane.

Back in the snow field Jim is on the radio.

'We're on the east ridge of Benmarochan five hundred metres from the trig point. Where are you Cooper?'

'Two miles from the summit but your friend is holding up well.'

'Come again? Who is holding up?'

'Jo.'

'What's she doing there?'

' Being a great help, of course.'

'Hold on, I hear the chopper....I see it. He's on course.'

The blades of the chopper noise increased. Jim held the radio and awaited contact.

'Recue 1 here. We need your exact location. Over'

'500 metres due east of the trig point on Benmagrochan. I'm waving a red vest. Over.

'Received and understood. ETA in three minutes. Stand by. Out.'

The helicopter landed 50m metres away on flat ground from the snow hole. The down force of the blades blew snow everywhere. Jim raised his arm to protect his face as the winch man ran towards him. He grabbed his arm.

'Where are the casualties?'

Jim pointed to the snow hole. Victoria was dragged out and a blanket wrapped round her. She managed to walk to the helicopter with the winch man. He returned with a second crew member to place Edward on a stretcher. He was then taken on board. The winch man then bent down to Tam. He examined him for any sign of life.

At the helicopter, Jim spoke to Victoria.

'What did Tam say to you dear?'

Victoria at first shrugged her shoulders.

'Oh he did say he would be ok with his fingers like this.' She demonstrated the sign.

'Then he put us in his jacket.'

Jim turned to walk away.

'He said one other thing.'

'Did he? Whit?' tell Jim.

'There's a special offer on; two for the price of one.'

The significance of what she had said, hit him poignantly. He pulled back as he and Victoria saw the winch man make the sign of the Cross. He then made a salute and took Tam's jacket and placed it over his face, tucking the arms under his body. He got up and ran to the helicopter. Victoria realised Tam was dead and started to cry.

'No, oh no, no, no Tam,' she cried.

The helicopter doors closed. It rose steeply and headed towards Dumfries Royal Infirmary.

Cooper and Flynn arrived by Jim's side to see the helicopter fade into the distance. Both men look at Jim as he knelt between Tam and Jess. They take the stretcher and casualty bag from their backs. As they assembled the stretcher, Jo arrived.

'What do you wish to do then?' asked Corporal Flynn.

'We'll take Tam back tae the farm.'

Tears roll down Jim's face. Flynn and Cooper roll the casualty bag out alongside Tam. Jo approached Jim.

'Are you all right dear?'

No, I've jist lost twa mair friends.'

'May I examine Tam before you put him in the casualty bag?'

'Aye.'

Jo took out her stethoscope from her pocket and ran her hand up the inside of Tam's T Shirt. Several seconds elapsed. Then Jo gasps.

'Jim, he's still got a heartbeat. It's faint but it's there!'

Jim fumbled with his radio.

'Helicopter 1. Please return. Pick up casualty. Over.

'Give me a minute over.'

Jim keeps the radio to his ear as blankets are put around Tam and Jo massages his heart.

'Negative. Sorry insufficient fuel for return. Suggest you make alternative arrangements. Over.'

'Oh please return. He's just clingin' oan tae life. Please, over.'

'Repeat Negative. No fuel. Over and Out.'

CHAPTER TWELVE

A NEW LIFE FOR TAM

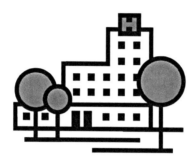

Dumfries & Galloway Royal Infirmary

Cooper and Flynn have Tam's body in the casualty bag. Jo put a tube down Tam's throat to aid his breathing by external manual application. Then Tam was then placed on a stretcher and securely fastened.

'We'll take him back to the farm.'

Jim radioed Bob.

'Bob, Tam is alive. Just alive but alive. We'll bring him down. Get the Land Rover ready, I'll run him tae hospital.'

'Great news. I'll get it ready.'

It took some time to get Tam off the hill. Jim guided them down and Cooper and Flynn did most of the stretcher work. Jess was due a burial where she lay abandoned in the snow.

The radio bleeped.

'Hi Bob.'

'Jim, the Land Rover is as dead as a duck. Can't get it started at all. No oil in the sump after last night's trip.

'Plan B then.'

'What's Plan B Jim?

'We'll have tae take Rupert's Range Rover. Bob. Get his back seats oot and the passenger wan tae.'

Bob went to search in a tool box with the radio at his ear.

'Ok Jim I'm oan tae it, over and out.'

Bob replaced his phone in his pocket and continued to rumble about. Rupert took an interest in what he's doing.

'What are you doing Bob?' he asked.

'The Land Rover has broken down and we need to take Tam tae hospital. Sorry mate but yours is the only car, an' tae fit the stretcher we'll hiv tae take the back seats oot.

'No way! You can't drive down the road anyway. It's blocked. I had also packed the car ready to be off once the weather cleared.

Bob ignored Rupert and took his tool box out into the snow trodden courtyard. Bob removed the back seats easily and took a little longer to unbolt the front passenger seat from the floorboards. He had no sooner finished when out of the side of his sight he saw the injured party approach.

'Here they come, Rupert.'

Rupert looked on with gritted teeth and a piercing stare. As he realised there was no alternative than to use his beautiful, and expensive, Range Rover.

'So Jim. What will ye dae?'

'I'm goan tae drive this off the hill an' doon the glen tae the back road.'

'That's suicide, Jim!'

'I've got tae try. Remember he saved my life too.

Noo, I'm goan tae save his. I'm returnin' the favour, that's a''.

Bob hands to Jim, Tam's knife.

'What's that fur?'

'In case ye need tae cut the seat belt. It micht come in haundy.'

Bob inserts the knife into the CD slit.

'An' if ye need tae ken, ma will and deeds fur the farm is in the tap drawer o' my dresser.'

Jo approaches Jim and Bob. A tear is in her eye.

'Jim, don't do it, please.'

Jim came over to Jo and held her arms. His pleading eyes served his cause.

'You know I hive tae dae it darlin'. It's his only hope.'

Jim closed the car window and prepared to leave. The two SAS men went ahead to lift the yard gate off its hinges and pulled it out of Jim's path. Jim drove out of the yard and began a roller coaster ride through the snow. Sometimes he disappeared from view in the drifts in the field. His concentration was on edge as he feared a slip, a split moment when the car's tyres might fail to engage the surface and a skid occur. He drove up to the top of the hill and noticed a flashing yellow light. Jock was out in his JCB clearing snow from the road.

Jim put the range rover into gear and headed down a steep hill. Half way down, Jim lost control. The vehicle gathered momentum and began to go into a free fall, rolling and tumbling as it went. The Range Rover landed on its roof on the road behind Jock's JCB.

Jock got out of his vehicle and bounded through snow fearing the worst. He peered through the window and saw Jim with the stretcher beside him. Jim's face was covered with blood as he hung upside down in his seat. Jock gingerly placed his hand in the car to see if he was alive. As he did, Jim recovered and grabbed Jock's hand.

'Git the car on tae its wheels Jock.'

'Right away Jim.'

Jock reversed the JCB up to the Range Rover and put the giant vehicle's sturdy legs down in position. He brought the actor round to the car. He hooked a chain from the JCB to the Range Rover. He mounted the yellow JCB and started to lift it back on to its wheels. Jock went back to Jim's door to get him out. He was alarmed to see Jim take the knife from the CD player out. But Jim cut the safety air bag out of his steering wheel and cut the safety belt off only to find he was trapped by the legs between the door and the central console. Jim turned and looked at Jock.

'Get the bugger started.'

'I don't think the Range Rover is goin' anywhere Jim. Get the bastard started.'

Jock went to the front of the vehicle. He removed the bonnet, which was already buckled, and started to work on the engine. It did not take long to see the problem.

'We need a miracle tae get this started.'

'Why?'

'Well, somewhere up that hill yiv jist come doon, lies yer battery! It's no here!'

'Then git the battery fae the JCB quick.'

'Good idea.'

Jock dismantled the JCB battery and inserted it into the Range Rover engine compartment. He wired it up. Crossed his fingers and asked Jim to spark up.

'Wow, turn it aff! It's rubbin' somewhere.'

Jock got a metal bar and prised off the grill at the

front to ease the friction but water started to run out of the engine compartment. Jim fired up the engine again.

'Well done Jock, that's me movin' again.'

'Dinnae worry aboot the water. It's melted snaw!'

Jim drove off with a toot of his horn and finally reached the main road where there was some more traffic making slow progress. He struggled to keep the vehicle in a straight line. Concentrating on his driving with the occasional attempts to massage Tam's heart, thumping his lungs to encourage breathing. Jim continued to weave past the slower drivers who are amazed to see such a ramshackle vehicle travelling at such a speed. However his erratic driving did catch the eye of a patrolling police car. Suddenly the siren was sounding and Jim knew it was his vehicle which was attracting the concern. The traffic officer pulled alongside Jim.

'Pull over, sir.'

'Officer I can't stop. Injured party on board.'

The truth was that Jim also knew his brakes were failing. But his bravado worked.

'Then follow me, I'll give you an escort to the DGRI.'

His words were like music to Jim's ears. The Police car overtook Jim and with its blue lights flashing and siren disturbing the silent snowy day, they proceeded towards Dumfries. Jim continued to struggle with the wayward vehicle. But after a half hour's drive in which cars parted as they approached, Jim and the police car entered the Doonhamer's town. As they approached traffic lights, set firmly at red, Jim wondered if he would end up in the back of the police car.

But with the siren as loud as a ship's fog horn and the flashing lights of a west end musical, the police car proceeded through red and Jim followed knocking over the central bollard as he did. This collision caused his mounted rear wheel, which had gone through cartwheels of action, to fall off. Jim pushed the console button marked 'Diff Lock' and carried on the busy town streets with the front wheel on the opposite side off the ground. They approached another set of traffic lights and Jim cursed why Dumfries was over lit at street corners compared with other towns in the region. But the police car was as effective as ever and he simply followed on.

Just before the hospital grounds, Jim confronted a set of road works. The police car began to overtake. But a dumper truck pulled out between them. Jim had a split second to decide what action to take before he crashed to a halt in the side of the dumper.

So Jim took a sharp right turn and drove straight at a fence and hedge marking the hospital boundary. Evading trees and bushes designed to give peace and calm to recovering patients, Jim dodged about and entered the virgin snow of the far away car park. Such relief at being at the hospital took hold of Jim but his worry was how to stop the car. He approached the main entrance of the hospital only to find a fire engine was parked by the doorway. He weighed up the odds. Destroy a hospital wing or crash into the fire engine. He chose the latter.

Jim drove with increased loss of vision. Even the fire engine became a blur. Then the sudden impact hit.

Jim was aware he was at the hospital, he had delivered his patient and the job was done but all he remembered was an orange flash as the fire engine caught fire. The fire men were able to douse the flames quickly and others found Jim unconscious lying on top of Tam in his stretcher, oblivious to the trauma his body had experienced.

Three days later Jim was recovering in ward 9. He became aware as an angel approached. The angel sat down beside him and took his hand.

'Where am I?', he whispered.

'You are in hospital Jim,' said Jo.

Jim smiled and he tried to raise himself up.

'Relax. Take it easy Jim.'

'I wis only goan tae kiss you!' he said.

'There will be plenty time for that later my love.'

Jim relaxed. He thought for a moment.

'What aboot Tam? Where's Tam?'

'The last I heard was that he was fighting for his life. You should have seen them. Doctors and nurses were running around trying to keep him alive. But I warn you Jim. It looks bad for Tam.'

Jim threw back the covers and tried to get out of bed.

'No you stay where you are,' said Jo reassuringly.

A nurse approached.

'Now now, Jim McKenzie. Back into bed you go.'

Jim relaxed back in bed and pulled the covers over him.

'That's better. Now if you want anything just let me know.'

'Thanks nurse,' he said.

He waited till she left the ward.

'What a want she canna gie me,' said Jim.

And with that set in his mind he threw the covers back and sat up.

'I'm goan tae see Tam.'

The room seemed to be going round and round. Jim stood still to gain his bearings. Too late, the nurse returned and sat him down on the bed.

'He's got concussion,' she said.

Half an hour later Bob arrived at the ward to visit Jim.

'Hi Jim. How are ye?

'Fine an' a' the better tae hear ye Bob. Tell me how's Tam?'

'That's what a need tae see ye aboot. You'd better come wi' me Jim. Thirs a problem wi' Tam. C'mon, thirs wan o' they wheeled chairs. Let's git ye in it.'

With Jo's help Bob managed to get Jim seated with a rug over his lap. Jo pushed it with Bob following on behind. As they proceed along the corridor, they met Rupert and Suzanne at the ward where Edward and Victoria were being treated.

'Have you seen the mess of my Range Rover?'

Jim gave him a cold stare.

'Cars can be replaced. People cannae. Tam's here fightin' fur his life. That man took the coat aff his back tae keep yer twa weans alive! Then he lay across them to give them his body warmth. So that they would survive! A sacrifice'.

Rupert turned to look at Victoria who was crying but nodded in agreement to what Jim had said. Edward wakened. His parents turn to him. Meanwhile Jo wheeled Jim forward to meet the doctors treating Tam.

'How long had Tam stopped breathing?' enquired the consultant.

'He wis dead. Whin a got tae him thir wis nae breathin,' nae heartbeat at a'.'

'Tam is actually brain dead. He's not going to make it. He had the lowest body temperature that I've ever encountered in nearly forty years as an accident and emergency consultant.'

Jim looked at the peaceful Tam. The most peaceful this energetic man had perhaps ever known. It was a body, damaged in so many places but containing a spirit of rare fortitude.

'As his only known next of kin, you realise, it is only a machine now which can keep him temporarily alive. Do we have your permission, to turn the machine off?'

Jim had a tear in his eye. He looked at Bob and then to Jo for support. Bob nods his head then turns away. Jo looks at Jim with tears running down her face.

'It's time to let him go, Jim'

Jim looked at the consultant and nods his agreement. The doctor went over to the machine and turned it off. A steady beep, beep, beep turns to a constant humming tone.

Two days later Jim was released from hospital with a jar of sedatives to be taken if required. He was not to work for at least 10 days and had an appointment to see his GP when that period of time had elapsed.

The following day he wore a white shirt and looking in the mirror, seeing still the scars of his daring exploits on his face, he tied his black tie. He put on his suit jacket and took the crook from behind the front door. He opened the door and looked at the clean tractor and trailer which Bob had spent the previous afternoon cleaning. It was only fitting that Tam should have some dignity on the last of his earthly days.

As Jim approached the trailer, he patted the coffin.

'Fareweel ma freend. Life will niver be the same without ye. But Tam, I owe ma life tae ye an' I'll niver forget ye. God rest you, Tam. This, I'm sad tae say is yer very last journey.'

Jim's tractor kept a steady 10 miles per hour and eventually approached the village. Cars, tractors, vans, four wheeled motorbikes and the local police car all sat at the verge of the road like a guard of honour as the tractor approached the kirk. Jim drove the tractor and trailer close to the grave and stopped. He walked with his crook and made his way to the rear of the trailer where Bob was standing. They pulled out the pins on each side of the trailer and lowered it down gently to reveal the coffin. A local Dumfries Police Piper, Ewan Grierson, played a lament as the coffin was taken from the trailer to the graveside. There were no flowers on the simple coffin but instead, one clump of bell heather and a handful of soil and stones on the lid of the coffin. The coffin was gently removed from the vehicle and set on the ground. The pall bearers approached to lift the coffin. Bob and Jock were at the back; Sandy and Geordie Craig, Bob's neighbours, were in the middle with Jim and Sergeant Cooper at the front.

Jim stumbled in front of Rupert and his family. Rupert caught the coffin but Jim quickly recovered.

'Take yer haunds aff that coffin. You're nae guid enough tae touch that man's coffin,' Jim snarled.

The coffin was placed on top of the boards over the grave. The men took a step back and bowed respectfully. When Ewan ended his piped lament, Sergeant Cooper and Corporal Flynn came to attention. They presented arms and fired two sharp volleys of gun fire over the coffin. The shots echoed all round the glen. They stood back and the Reverend Gordon Savage MA BD began the funeral service.

The following day a brand new gold Range Rover Vogue 3.6 litre TDV 8 diesel with full leather interior, real wood facings, hard disc navigation, Bluetooth connectivity and full colour 12.3 inch instrument panel drove into Jim's court yard.

Jim was in his slippers but came out to see who it was. The proud driver opened his door and Rupert came out of it. He closed his car door gently.

'That's some car!'

'Well I had to get back to Surrey tomorrow somehow'.

'So where did ye get that amazing car?'

'Oh I had to go back to England. You don't seem to have a local Range Rover sales garage around here.'

'Oh ye mist hive been tae Lloyds in Carlisle then.'

'Spot on Jim. Jeremy Shankland, a delightful and most knowledgeable man, showed me around the sales room. He even gave me a few test drives in some of the cars on show. But I settled for this one. It's a real beauty. I'm looking forward to getting down to Surrey tomorrow in it.'

' Aye, I ken Jeremy, his mother stays in the next village. He wis always keen oan cars. But that must have set ye back a pretty penny.'

'Not really. It's the quality I pay for. Sixty-six thousand and every penny is worth it. You'd be more than happy upgrading your Land Rover.'

'Ma Land Rover is a work horse, no a family tourer. Anyway, come awa in. I wis wantin' a word with ye before ye went awa'. But a warn ye. Yer naw gonna like whit I've got tae say.'

'Whatever next!'

'Ye se, Tam always hud a sleepin' bag in its case, in his rucksack.

'So?'

'Well, oan that dreadful day whin Tam went up tae the hill, he hud his rucksack wi' him but nae sleepin' bag.'

'What are you implying?'

'Cooper and Flynn went tae look for it an' foond it wis oan your son's bed in the bothy.'

Rupert placed his hand on his head and scratched it.

'But why did Tam know to go after them?'

'It wis like this. He telt them where they'd get a good signal for their phone tae text and when they didnae come back, Tam felt a responsibility an' took it oan him sel' tae go an' find them before they a' died in the snaw.'

Jim pointed his finger at Rupert.

'It should be you! There's a man lyin' six feet under in a grave because your children wanted tae mak insignificant phone calls and texts. A heavy price tae pay don't ye think?'

Rupert shook in a guilty shiver. He got up to leave. He had heard enough from Jim.

'Rupert, before ye go, promise me wan thing.'

'What's that?'

'Promise never tae tell yer son aboot Tam's sleepin' bag, which you geed him.

'Why?'

'Because he's gonna hae this hingin' o'er him fur the rest o' his life. So let's leave it jist between you an' me. OK?'

Rupert left Jim's house and went back to his brand new Range Rover Vogue. Rupert lowered his window electronically, and waved farewell. Jim raised his arm and gave a final wave. As Rupert drove off, Jim saw his brake lights come on. Another car was approaching. Jo stopped and conversed briefly with Rupert while Jim rushed back into the house to put his shoes on.

'Hello, are you in?'

'Yes darling, I'm comin'.'

'Well, is that them away?'

'Aye will be awa in a few minutes. Good riddance as they say.'

'Don't say that Jim. Come here.'

She gave him a hug.

'Anyway I've got a surprise for you.'

'I dinnae deserve ony surprises.'

Jim pulled himself away and looked at Jo. He wondered what was on her mind.

'Whit hav ye got there?'

Jo lifted a border collie pup out of the back of her car. Jim was surprised and delighted. As he took the pup out of Jo's hands he held it up in front of himself. His spirits were lifted too.

'So whits yer name ma wee fella?'

'Well spotted. It is a boy this time.'

'Then I'll call him..... Tam. Aye he must be Tam.'

'Right I'll start making tea for three of us this evening.'

'Have ye ony rabbit in the car fur me tae skin?'

No, I've got roast chicken this evening. Easy preparation, you might say.

'It is in your haunds onyway,' he laughed.

Jim placed the dog on the floor. He looked at his movement and smiled.

Well then. I'm goan tae gie the wee fella his first walk oan the hill. Come oan Tam. Let's go fur a wee walkie. Jim picked up his crook, picked up Tam in his arms and set off up the hill.

They proceeded up the hill with Tam bounding ahead then looking back always to see where his master was. Jim picked him up and gave him a cuddle. He put him down again.

'This is whur ye will be workin' Tam.'

The mist was gathering at the top of the field. Tam let out a yelp as he looked ahead of himself.

'What's that that ye see, ma wee man?'

Jim looked over his right shoulder. He saw a lone figure in the distance covered with mist. The outline got closer. He saw a masked man walk on the hill. The figure stopped and looked at Jim. Jim waved at the man. There was an uncanny resemblance to Big Tam in his mind. The man waved back then purposefully walked on up the hill and into the mist. Then he was gone from sight. Jim smiled. Was his imagination getting the better of him or was it just possible that the spirit of Big Tam was still around?

Jo's chicken would soon be ready.

'An' I think there will be a wee bit left fur you, ma wee leeze.'

Jim turned around. Tam immediately followed his heel. A broad smile came across Jim's face. Life was improving beyond his wildest dreams. He could almost convince himself that Jo's roast chicken was in his nostrils. It was certainly in young Tam's.

The End.

Books by Miller Caldwell

Novels
Operation Oboe
Restless Waves
Betrayed in the Nith
The Last Shepherd

Biographies
Untied Laces. His autobiography
NB A LARGE PRINT coloured edition of Untied Laces can be found in the Ewart Library Loans Section, Dumfries.
Poet's Progeny- The descendants of the Bard
7 point 7 on the Richter scale – diary of the Camp Manager at Mundihar NWFP of Pakistan.

Self Help Books
Have You Seen My...Ummm...Memory?
Ponderings (poems and short stories for restricted sight.)
It's Me, Honest it is (NHS Booklet)

Contact the author for signed copies - Ideal gifts!
mhcaldwell@btopenworld
www.millercaldwell.org

Lightning Source UK Ltd.
Milton Keynes UK
14 January 2011
165744UK00001B/4/P